Contributions to All The Year Round

Charles Dickens

Contents

CONTRIBUTIONS TO ALL THE YEAR ROUND

BY

Charles Dickens

ANNOUNCEMENT IN "HOUSEHOLD WORDS" OF THE APPROACHING PUBLICATION OF "ALL THE YEAR ROUND"

After the appearance of the present concluding Number of Household Words, this publication will merge into the new weekly publication, All the Year Round, and the title, Household Words, will form a part of the title-page of All the Year Round.

The Prospectus of the latter Journal describes it in these words:

"ADDRESS

"Nine years of Household Words, are the best practical assurance that can be offered to the public, of the spirit and objects of All the Year Round.

"In transferring myself, and my strongest energies, from the publication that is about to be discontinued, to the publication that is about to be begun, I have the happiness of taking with me the staff of writers with whom I have laboured, and all the literary and business co-operation that can make my work a pleasure. In some important respects, I am now free greatly to advance on past arrangements. Those, I leave to testify for themselves in due course.

"That fusion of the graces of the imagination with the realities of life, which is vital to the welfare of any community, and for which I have striven from week to week as honestly as I could during the last nine years, will continue to be striven for "all the year round". The old weekly cares and duties become things of the Past, merely to be assumed, with an increased love for them and brighter hopes springing out of them, in the Present and the Future.

"I look, and plan, for a very much wider circle of readers, and yet again for a steadily expanding circle of readers, in the projects I hope to carry through "all the year round". And I feel confident that this expectation will be realized, if it deserve realization.

"The task of my new journal is set, and it will steadily try to work the task out. Its pages shall show to what good purpose their motto is remembered in them, and with how much of fidelity and earnestness they tell

"the story of our lives from year to year.

"CHARLES DICKENS."

Since this was issued, the Journal itself has come into existence, and has spoken for itself five weeks. Its fifth Number is published to-day, and its circulation, moderately stated, trebles that now relinquished in Household Words.

In referring our readers, henceforth, to All the Year Round, we can but assure them afresh, of our unwearying and faithful service, in what is at once the work and the chief pleasure of our life. Through all that we are doing, and through all that we design to do, our aim is to do our best in sincerity of purpose, and true devotion of spirit.

We do not for a moment suppose that we may lean on the character of these pages, and rest contented at the point where they stop. We see in that point but a starting-place for our new journey; and on that journey, with new prospects opening out before us everywhere, we joyfully proceed, entreating our readers--without any of the pain of leave-taking incidental to most journeys--to bear us company All the year round.

Saturday, May 28, 1859.

THE POOR MAN AND HIS BEER

My friend Philosewers and I, contemplating a farm-labourer the other day, who was drinking his mug of beer on a settle at a roadside ale-house door, we fell to humming the fag-end of an old ditty, of which the poor man and his beer, and the sin of parting them, form the doleful burden. Philosewers then mentioned to me that a friend of his in an agricultural county--say a Hertfordshire friend--had, for two years last past, endeavoured to reconcile the poor man and his beer to public morality, by making it a point of honour between himself and the poor man that the latter should use his beer and not abuse it. Interested in an effort of so unobtrusive and unspeechifying a nature, "O Philosewers," said I, after the manner of the dreary sages in Eastern apologues, "Show me, I pray, the man who deems that temperance can be attained without a medal, an oration, a banner, and a denunciation of half the world, and who has at once the head and heart to set about it!"

Philosewers expressing, in reply, his willingness to gratify the dreary sage, an appointment was made for the purpose. And on the day fixed, I, the Dreary one, accompanied by Philosewers, went down Nor'-West per railway, in search of temperate temperance. It was a thunderous day; and the clouds were so immoderately watery, and so very much disposed to sour all the beer in Hertfordshire, that they seemed to have taken the pledge.

But, the sun burst forth gaily in the afternoon, and gilded the old gables, and old mullioned windows, and old weathercock and old clock-face, of the quaint old house which is the dwelling of the man we sought. How shall I describe him? As one of the most famous practical chemists of the age? That designation will do as well as another--better, perhaps, than most others. And his name? Friar Bacon.

"Though, take notice, Philosewers," said I, behind my hand, "that the first Friar

Bacon had not that handsome lady-wife beside him. Wherein, O Philosewers, he was a chemist, wretched and forlorn, compared with his successor. Young Romeo bade the holy father Lawrence hang up philosophy, unless philosophy could make a Juliet. Chemistry would infallibly be hanged if its life were staked on making anything half so pleasant as this Juliet." The gentle Philosewers smiled assent.

The foregoing whisper from myself, the Dreary one, tickled the ear of Philosewers, as we walked on the trim garden terrace before dinner, among the early leaves and blossoms; two peacocks, apparently in very tight new boots, occasionally crossing the gravel at a distance. The sun, shining through the old house-windows, now and then flashed out some brilliant piece of colour from bright hangings within, or upon the old oak panelling; similarly, Friar Bacon, as we paced to and fro, revealed little glimpses of his good work.

"It is not much," said he. "It is no wonderful thing. There used to be a great deal of drunkenness here, and I wanted to make it better if I could. The people are very ignorant, and have been much neglected, and I wanted to make THAT better, if I could. My utmost object was, to help them to a little self-government and a little homely pleasure. I only show the way to better things, and advise them. I never act for them; I never interfere; above all, I never patronise."

I had said to Philosewers as we came along Nor'-West that patronage was one of the curses of England; I appeared to rise in the estimation of Philosewers when thus confirmed.

"And so," said Friar Bacon, "I established my Allotment-club, and my pig-clubs, and those little Concerts by the ladies of my own family, of which we have the last of the season this evening. They are a great success, for the people here are amazingly fond of music. But there is the early dinner-bell, and I have no need to talk of my endeavours when you will soon see them in their working dress".

Dinner done, behold the Friar, Philosewers, and myself the Dreary one, walking, at six o'clock, across the fields, to the "Club- house."

As we swung open the last field-gate and entered the Allotment- grounds, many members were already on their way to the Club, which stands in the midst of the allotments. Who could help thinking of the wonderful contrast between these club-men and the club-men of St. James's Street, or Pall Mall, in London! Look at yonder prematurely old man, doubled up with work, and leaning on a rude stick more crooked than himself, slowly trudging to the club-house, in a shapeless hat like an Italian harlequin's, or an old brown- paper bag, leathern leggings, and dull green smock-frock, looking as though duck-weed had accumulated on it--the result of its stagnant life--or as if it were a vegetable production, originally meant to blow into something better, but stopped somehow. Compare him with Old Cousin Feenix, ambling along St. James's Street, got up in the style of a couple of generations ago, and with a head of hair, a complexion, and a set of teeth, profoundly impossible to be believed in by the widest stretch of human credulity. Can they both be men and brothers? Verily they are. And although Cousin Feenix has lived so fast that he will die at Baden-Baden, and although this club-man in the frock has lived, ever since he came to man's estate, on nine shillings a week, and is sure to die in the Union if he die in bed, yet he brought as much into the world as Cousin Feenix, and will take as much out--more, for more of him is real.

A pretty, simple building, the club-house, with a rustic colonnade outside, under which the members can sit on wet evenings, looking at the patches of ground they cultivate for themselves; within, a well- ventilated room, large and lofty, cheerful pavement of coloured tiles, a bar for serving out the beer, good supply of forms and chairs, and a brave big chimney-corner, where the fire burns cheerfully. Adjoining this room, another:

"Built for a reading-room," said Friar Bacon; "but not much used-- yet."

The dreary sage, looking in through the window, perceiving a fixed reading-desk within, and inquiring its use:

"I have Service there," said Friar Bacon. "They never went anywhere to hear prayers, and of course it would be hopeless to help them to be happier and better, if they had no religious feeling at all."

"The whole place is very pretty." Thus the sage.

"I am glad you think so. I built it for the holders of the Allotment-grounds, and gave it them: only requiring them to manage it by a committee of their own appointing, and never to get drunk there. They never have got drunk there."

"Yet they have their beer freely?"

"O yes. As much as they choose to buy. The club gets its beer direct from the brewer, by the barrel. So they get it good; at once much cheaper, and much better, than at the public-house. The members take it in turns to be steward, and serve out the beer: if a man should decline to serve when his turn came, he would pay a fine of twopence. The steward lasts, as long as the barrel lasts. When there is a new barrel, there is a new steward."

"What a noble fire is roaring up that chimney!"

"Yes, a capital fire. Every member pays a halfpenny a week."

"Every member must be the holder of an Allotment-garden?"

"Yes; for which he pays five shillings a year. The Allotments you see about us, occupy some sixteen or eighteen acres, and each garden is as large as experience shows one man to be able to manage. You see how admirably they are tilled, and how much they get off them. They are always working in them in their spare hours; and when a man wants a mug of beer, instead of going off to the village and the public-house, he puts down his spade or his hoe, comes to the club- house and gets it, and goes back to his work. When he has done work, he likes to have his beer at the club, still, and to sit and look at his little crops as they thrive."

"They seem to manage the club very well."

"Perfectly well. Here are their own rules. They made them. I never interfere with them, except to advise them when they ask me."

RULES AND REGULATIONS MADE BY THE COMMITTEE From the 21st September, 1857

One half-penny per week to be paid to the club by each member

1.--Each member to draw the beer in order, according to the number of his allotment; on failing, a forfeit of twopence to be paid to the club.

2.--The member that draws the beer to pay for the same, and bring his ticket up receipted when the subscriptions are paid; on failing to do so, a penalty of sixpence to be forfeited and paid to the club.

3.--The subscriptions and forfeits to be paid at the club-room on the last Saturday night of each month.

4.--The subscriptions and forfeits to be cleared up every quarter; if not, a penalty of sixpence to be paid to the club.

5.--The member that draws the beer to be at the club-room by six o'clock every evening, and stay till ten; but in the event of no member being there, he may leave at nine; on failing so to attend, a penalty of sixpence to be paid to the club.

6.--Any member giving beer to a stranger in this club-room, excepting to his wife or family, shall be liable to the penalty of one shilling.

7.--Any member lifting his hand to strike another in this club-room shall be liable to the penalty of sixpence.

8.--Any member swearing in this club-room shall be liable to a penalty of two-pence each time.

9.--Any member selling beer shall be expelled from the club.

10.--Any member wishing to give up his allotment, may apply to the committee, and they shall value the crop and the condition of the ground. The amount of the valuation shall be paid by the succeeding tenant, who shall be allowed to enter on any part of the allotment which is uncropped at the time of notice of the leaving tenant.

11.--Any member not keeping his allotment-garden clear from seed- weeds, or otherwise injuring his neighbours, may be turned out of his garden by the votes of two-thirds of the committee, one month's notice being given to him.

12.--Any member carelessly breaking a mug, is to pay the cost of replacing the same.

I was soliciting the attention of Philosewers to some old old bonnets hanging in the Allotment-gardens to frighten the birds, and the fashion of which I should think would terrify a French bird to death at any distance, when Philosewers solicited my attention to the scrapers at the club-house door. The amount of the soil of England which every member brought there on his feet, was indeed surprising; and even I, who am professedly a salad-eater, could have grown a salad for my dinner, in the earth on any member's frock or hat.

"Now," said Friar Bacon, looking at his watch, "for the Pig-clubs!"

The dreary Sage entreated explanation.

"Why, a pig is so very valuable to a poor labouring man, and it is so very difficult for him at this time of the year to get money enough to buy one, that I lend him a pound for the purpose. But, I do it in this way. I leave such of the club members as choose it and desire it, to form themselves into parties of five. To every man in each company of five, I lend a pound, to buy a pig. But, each man of the five becomes bound for every other man, as to the repayment of his money. Consequently, they look after one another, and pick out their partners with care; selecting men in whom they have confidence."

"They repay the money, I suppose, when the pig is fattened, killed, and sold?"

"Yes. Then they repay the money. And they do repay it. I had one man, last year, who was a little tardy (he was in the habit of going to the public-house); but even he did pay. It is an immense Advantage to one of these poor fellows to have a pig. The pig consumes the refuse from the man's cottage and allotment-garden, and the pig's refuse enriches the man's garden besides. The pig is the poor man's friend. Come into the club-house again."

The poor man's friend. Yes. I have often wondered who really was the poor man's friend among a great number of competitors, and I now clearly perceive him to be the pig. HE never makes any flourishes about the poor man. HE never gammons the poor man--except to his manifest advantage in the article of bacon. HE never comes down to this house, or goes down to his constituents. He openly declares to the poor man, "I want my sty because I am a Pig. I desire to have as much to eat as you can by any means stuff me with, because I am a Pig." HE never gives the poor man a sovereign for bringing up a family. HE never grunts the poor man's name in vain. And when he dies in the odour of Porkity, he cuts up, a highly useful creature and a blessing to the poor man, from the ring in his snout to the curl in his tail. Which of the poor man's other friends can say as much? Where is the M.P. who means Mere Pork?

The dreary Sage had glided into these reflections, when he found himself sitting by the club-house fire, surrounded by green smock- frocks and shapeless hats: with Friar Bacon lively, busy, and expert, at a little table near him.

"Now, then, come. The first five!" said Friar Bacon. "Where are you?"

"Order!" cried a merry-faced little man, who had brought his young daughter with him to see life, and who always modestly hid his face in his beer-mug after he had thus assisted the business.

"John Nightingale, William Thrush, Joseph Blackbird, Cecil Robin, and Thomas Linnet!" cried Friar Bacon.

"Here, sir!" and "Here, sir!" And Linnet, Robin, Blackbird, Thrush, and Nightingale, stood confessed.

We, the undersigned, declare, in effect, by this written paper, that each of us is responsible for the repayment of this pig-money by each of the other. "Sure you understand, Nightingale?"

"Ees, sur."

"Can you write your name, Nightingale?"

"Na, sur."

Nightingale's eye upon his name, as Friar Bacon wrote it, was a sight to consider in after years. Rather incredulous was Nightingale, with a hand at the corner of his mouth, and his head on one side, as to those drawings really meaning him. Doubtful was Nightingale whether any virtue had gone out of him in that committal to paper. Meditative was Nightingale as to what would come of young Nightingale's growing up to the acquisition of that art. Suspended was the interest of Nightingale, when his name was done--as if he thought the letters were only sown, to come up presently in some other form. Prodigious, and wrong-handed was the cross made by Nightingale on much encouragement--the strokes directed from him instead of towards him; and most patient and sweet-humoured was the smile of Nightingale as he stepped back into a general laugh.

"Order!" cried the little man. Immediately disappearing into his mug.

"Ralph Mangel, Roger Wurzel, Edward Vetches, Matthew Carrot, and Charles Taters!" said Friar Bacon.

"All here, sir."

"You understand it, Mangel?"

"Iss, sir, I unnerstaans it."

"Can you write your name, Mangel?"

"Iss, sir."

Breathless interest. A dense background of smock-frocks accumulated behind Mangel, and many eyes in it looked doubtfully at Friar Bacon, as who should say, "Can he really though?" Mangel put down his hat, retired a little to get a good look at the paper, wetted his right hand thoroughly by drawing it slowly across his mouth, approached the paper with great determination, flattened it, sat down at it, and got well to his work. Circuitous and sea-serpent-like, were the movements of the tongue of Mangel while he formed the letters; elevated were the eyebrows of Mangel and sidelong the eyes, as, with his left whisker reposing on his left arm, they followed his performance; many were the misgivings of Mangel, and slow was his retrospective meditation touching the junction of the letter p with h; something too active was the big forefinger of Mangel in its propensity to rub out without proved cause. At last, long and deep was the breath drawn by Mangel when he laid down the pen; long and deep the wondering breath drawn by the background--as if they had watched his walking across the rapids of Niagara, on stilts, and now cried, "He has done it!"

But, Mangel was an honest man, if ever honest man lived. "T'owt to be a hell, sir," said he, contemplating his work, "and I ha' made a t on 't."

The over-fraught bosoms of the background found relief in a roar of laughter.

"OR-DER!" cried the little man. "CHEER!" And after that second word, came forth from his mug no more.

Several other clubs signed, and received their money. Very few could write their names; all who could not, pleaded that they could not, more or less sorrowfully, and always with a shake of the head, and in a lower voice than their natural speaking voice. Crosses could be made standing; signatures must be sat down to. There was no exception to this rule. Meantime, the various club-members smoked, drank their beer, and talked together quite unrestrained. They all wore their hats, except when they went up to Friar Bacon's table. The merry-faced little man offered his beer, with a natural good-fellowship, both to the Dreary one and Philosewers. Both partook of it with thanks.

"Seven o'clock!" said Friar Bacon. "And now we better get across to the concert, men, for the music will be beginning."

The concert was in Friar Bacon's laboratory; a large building near at hand, in an open field. The bettermost people of the village and neighbourhood were in a gallery on one side, and, in a gallery opposite the orchestra. The whole space below was filled with the labouring people and their families, to the number of five or six hundred. We had been obliged to turn away two hundred to-night, Friar Bacon said, for want of room--and that, not counting the boys, of whom we had taken in only a few picked ones, by reason of the boys, as a class, being given to too fervent a custom of applauding with their boot-heels.

The performers were the ladies of Friar Bacon's family, and two gentlemen; one of them, who presided, a Doctor of Music. A piano was the only instrument. Among the vocal pieces, we had a negro melody (rapturously encored), the Indian Drum, and the Village Blacksmith; neither did we want for fashionable Italian, having Ah! non giunge, and Mi manca la voce. Our success was splendid; our good-humoured, unaffected, and modest bearing, a pattern. As to the audience, they were far more polite and far more pleased than at the Opera; they were faultless. Thus for barely an hour the concert lasted, with thousands of great bottles looking on from the walls, containing the results of Friar Bacon's Million and one experiments in agricultural chemistry; and containing too, no doubt, a variety of materials with which the Friar could have blown us all through the roof at five minutes' notice.

God save the Queen being done, the good Friar stepped forward and said a few words, more particularly concerning two points; firstly, that Saturday half-holiday, which it would be kind in farmers to grant; secondly, the additional Allotment-grounds we were going to establish, in consequence of the happy success of the system, but which we could not guarantee should entitle the holders to be members of the club, because the present members must consider and settle that question for themselves: a bargain between man and man being always a bargain, and we having made over the club to them as the original Allotment-men. This was loudly applauded, and so, with contented and affectionate cheering, it was all over.

As Philosewers, and I the Dreary, posted back to London, looking up at the moon and discussing it as a world preparing for the habitation of responsible creatures, we expatiated on the honour due to men in this world of ours who try to prepare it for a higher course, and to leave the race who live and die upon it better than they found them.

FIVE NEW POINTS OF CRIMINAL LAW

The existing Criminal Law has been found in trials for Murder, to be so exceedingly hasty, unfair, and oppressive--in a word, to be so very objectionable to the amiable persons accused of that thoughtless act--that it is, we understand, the intention of the Government to bring in a Bill for its amendment. We have been favoured with an outline of its probable provisions.

It will be grounded on the profound principle that the real offender is the Murdered Person; but for whose obstinate persistency in being murdered, the interesting fellow-creature to be tried could not have got into trouble.

Its leading enactments may be expected to resolve themselves under the following heads:

1. There shall be no judge. Strong representations have been made by highly popular culprits that the presence of this obtrusive character is prejudicial to their best interests. The Court will be composed of a political gentleman, sitting in a secluded room commanding a view of St. James's Park, who has already more to do than any human creature can, by any stretch of the human imagination, be supposed capable of doing.

2. The jury to consist of Five Thousand Five Hundred and Fifty-five Volunteers.

3. The jury to be strictly prohibited from seeing either the accused or the witnesses. They are not to be sworn. They are on no account to hear the evidence. They are to receive it, or such representations of it, as may happen to fall in their way; and they will constantly write letters about it to all the Papers.

4. Supposing the trial to be a trial for Murder by poisoning, and supposing the hypothetical case, or the evidence, for the prosecution to charge the administration of two poisons, say Arsenic and Antimony; and supposing the taint of Arsenic in the

body to be possible but not probable, and the presence of Antimony in the body, to be an absolute certainty; it will then become the duty of the jury to confine their attention solely to the Arsenic, and entirely to dismiss the Antimony from their minds.

5. The symptoms preceding the death of the real offender (or Murdered Person) being described in evidence by medical practitioners who saw them, other medical practitioners who never saw them shall be required to state whether they are inconsistent with certain known diseases--but, THEY SHALL NEVER BE ASKED WHETHER THEY ARE NOT EXACTLY CONSISTENT WITH THE ADMINIS-TRATION OF POISON. To illustrate this enactment in the proposed Bill by a case:-A raging mad dog is seen to run into the house where Z lives alone, foaming at the mouth. Z and the mad dog are for some time left together in that house under proved circumstances, irresistibly leading to the conclusion that Z has been bitten by the dog. Z is afterwards found lying on his bed in a state of hydrophobia, and with the marks of the dog's teeth. Now, the symptoms of that disease being identical with those of another disease called Tetanus, which might supervene on Z's running a rusty nail into a certain part of his foot, medical practitioners who never saw Z, shall bear testimony to that abstract fact, and it shall then be incumbent on the Registrar-General to certify that Z died of a rusty nail.

It is hoped that these alterations in the present mode of procedure will not only be quite satisfactory to the accused person (which is the first great consideration), but will also tend, in a tolerable degree, to the welfare and safety of society. For it is not sought in this moderate and prudent measure to be wholly denied that it is an inconvenience to Society to be poisoned overmuch.

LEIGH HUNT: A REMONSTRANCE

The sense of beauty and gentleness, of moral beauty and faithful gentleness, grew upon him as the clear evening closed in. When he went to visit his relative at Putney, he still carried with him his work, and the books he more immediately wanted. Although his bodily powers had been giving way, his most conspicuous qualities, his memory for books, and his affection remained; and when his hair was white, when his ample chest had grown slender, when the very proportion of his height had visibly lessened, his step was still ready, and his dark eyes brightened at every happy expression, and at every thought of kindness. His death was simply exhaustion; he broke off his work to lie down and repose. So gentle was the final approach, that he scarcely recognised it till the very last, and then it came without terrors. His physical suffering had not been severe; at the latest hour he said that his only uneasiness was failing breath. And that failing breath was used to express his sense of the inexhaustible kindness he had received from the family who had been so unexpectedly made his nurses,--to draw from one of his sons, by minute, eager, and searching questions, all that he could learn about the latest vicissitudes and growing hopes of Italy,--to ask the friends and children around him for news of those whom he loved,--and to send love and messages to the absent who loved him."

Thus, with a manly simplicity and filial affection, writes the eldest son of Leigh Hunt in recording his father's death. These are the closing words of a new edition of The Autobiography of Leigh Hunt, published by Messrs. Smith and Elder, of Cornhill, revised by that son, and enriched with an introductory chapter of remarkable beauty and tenderness. The son's first presentation of his father to the reader, "rather tall, straight as an arrow, looking slenderer than he really was; his hair black and shining, and slightly inclined to wave; his head high, his forehead straight and white, his eyes black and sparkling, his general complexion dark; in his whole car-riage and manner an extraordinary degree of life," completes the picture. It is the picture of the flourishing and fading away of man that is born of a woman and hath but a short time to live.

In his presentation of his father's moral nature and intellectual qualities, Mr Hunt is no less faithful and no less touching. Those who knew Leigh Hunt, will see the bright face and hear the musical voice again, when he is recalled to them in this passage: "Even at seasons of the greatest depression in his fortunes, he always attracted many visitors, but still not so much for any repute that attended him as for his personal qualities. Few men were more attractive, in society, whether in a large company or over the fireside. His manners were peculiarly animated; his conversation, varied, ranging over a great field of subjects, was moved and called forth by the response of his companion, be that companion philosopher or student, sage or boy, man or woman; and he was equally ready for the most lively topics or for the gravest reflections--his expression easily adapting itself to the tone of his companion's mind. With much freedom of manners, he combined a spontaneous courtesy that never failed, and a considerateness derived from a ceaseless kindness of heart that invariably fascinated even strangers." Or in this: "His animation, his sympathy with what was gay and pleasurable; his avowed doctrine of cultivating cheerfulness, were manifest on the surface, and could be appreciated by those who knew him in society, most probably even exaggerated as salient traits, on which he himself insisted WITH A SORT OF GAY AND OSTENTATIOUS WILFULNESS."

The last words describe one of the most captivating peculiarities of a most orig-inal and engaging man, better than any other words could. The reader is besought to observe them, for a reason that shall presently be given. Lastly: "The anxiety to recognise the right of others, the tendency to 'refine', which was noted by an early school companion, and the propensity to elaborate every thought, made him, along with the direct argument by which he sustained his own conviction, recognise and almost admit all that might be said on the opposite side". For these reasons, and for others suggested with equal felicity, and with equal fidelity, the son writes of the father, "It is most desirable that his qualities should be known as they were; for such deficiencies as he had are the honest explanation of his mistakes; while, as the read-er may see from his writings and his conduct, they are not, as the faults of which he was accused would be, incompatible with the noblest faculties both of head and heart. To know Leigh Hunt as he was, was to hold him in reverence and love."

These quotations are made here, with a special object. It is not, that the personal testimony of one who knew Leigh Hunt well, may be borne to their truthfulness. It is not, that it may be recorded in these pages, as in his son's introductory chapter, that his life was of the most amiable and domestic kind, that his wants were few, that his way of life was frugal, that he was a man of small expenses, no ostentations, a diligent labourer, and a secluded man of letters. It is not, that the inconsiderate and forgetful may be reminded of his wrongs and sufferings in the days of the Regency, and of the national disgrace of his imprisonment. It is not, that their forbearance may be entreated for his grave, in right of his graceful fancy or his political labours and endurances, though -

Not only we, the latest seed of Time, New men, that in the flying of a wheel Cry down the past, not only we, that prate Of rights and wrongs, have loved the people well.

It is, that a duty may be done in the most direct way possible. An act of plain, clear duty.

Four or five years ago, the writer of these lines was much pained by accidentally encountering a printed statement, "that Mr. Leigh Hunt was the original of Harold Skimpole in Bleak House". The writer of these lines, is the author of that book. The statement came from America. It is no disrespect to that country, in which the writer has, perhaps, as many friends and as true an interest as any man that lives, good-humouredly to state the fact, that he has, now and then, been the subject of paragraphs in Transatlantic newspapers, more surprisingly destitute of all foundation in truth than the wildest delusions of the wildest lunatics. For reasons born of this experience, he let the thing go by.

But, since Mr. Leigh Hunt's death, the statement has been revived in England. The delicacy and generosity evinced in its revival, are for the rather late consideration of its revivers. The fact is this:

Exactly those graces and charms of manner which are remembered in the words we have quoted, were remembered by the author of the work of fiction in question, when he drew the character in question. Above all other things, that "sort of gay and ostentatious wilfulness" in the humouring of a subject, which had many a time delighted him, and impressed him as being unspeakably whimsical and attractive, was the airy quality he wanted for the man he invented. Partly for this reason, and partly (he has since often grieved to think) for the pleasure it afforded him to find that delightful manner reproducing itself under his hand, he yielded to the temptation of too often making the character SPEAK like his old friend. He no more thought, God forgive him! that the admired original would ever be charged with the imaginary vices of the fictitious creature, than he has himself ever thought of charging the blood of Desdemona and Othello, on the innocent Academy model who sat for Iago's leg in the picture. Even as to the mere occasional manner, he meant to be so cautious and conscientious, that he privately referred the proof sheets of the first number of that book to two intimate literary friends of Leigh Hunt (both still living), and altered the whole of that part of the text on their discovering too strong a resemblance to his "way".

He cannot see the son lay this wreath on the father's tomb, and leave him to the possibility of ever thinking that the present words might have righted the father's memory and were left unwritten. He cannot know that his own son may have to explain his father when folly or malice can wound his heart no more, and leave this task undone.

THE TATTLESNIVEL BLEATER

The pen is taken in hand on the present occasion, by a private individual (not wholly unaccustomed to literary composition), for the exposure of a conspiracy of a most frightful nature; a conspiracy which, like the deadly Upas-tree of Java, on which the individual produced a poem in his earlier youth (not wholly devoid of length), which was so flatteringly received (in circles not wholly unaccustomed to form critical opinions), that he was recommended to publish it, and would certainly have carried out the suggestion, but for private considerations (not wholly unconnected with expense).

The individual who undertakes the exposure of the gigantic conspiracy now to be laid bare in all its hideous deformity, is an inhabitant of the town of Tattlesnivel--a lowly inhabitant, it may be, but one who, as an Englishman and a man, will ne'er abase his eye before the gaudy and the mocking throng.

Tattlesnivel stoops to demand no championship from her sons. On an occasion in History, our bluff British monarch, our Eighth Royal Harry, almost went there. And long ere the periodical in which this exposure will appear, had sprung into being, Tattlesnivel had unfurled that standard which yet waves upon her battlements. The standard alluded to, is THE TATTLESNIVEL BLEATER, containing the latest intelligence, and state of markets, down to the hour of going to press, and presenting a favourable local medium for advertisers, on a graduated scale of charges, considerably diminishing in proportion to the guaranteed number of insertions.

It were bootless to expatiate on the host of talent engaged in formidable phalanx to do fealty to the Bleater. Suffice it to select, for present purposes, one of the most gifted and (but for the wide and deep ramifications of an un-English conspiracy) most rising, of the men who are bold Albion's pride. It were needless, after this preamble, to point the finger more directly at the LONDON CORRESPONDENT

OF THE TATTLESNIVEL BLEATER.

On the weekly letters of that Correspondent, on the flexibility of their English, on the boldness of their grammar, on the originality of their quotations (never to be found as they are printed, in any book existing), on the priority of their information, on their intimate acquaintance with the secret thoughts and unexecuted intentions of men, it would ill become the humble Tattlesnivellian who traces these words, to dwell. They are graven in the memory; they are on the Bleater's file. Let them be referred to.

But from the infamous, the dark, the subtle conspiracy which spreads its baleful roots throughout the land, and of which the Bleater's London Correspondent is the one sole subject, it is the purpose of the lowly Tattlesnivellian who undertakes this revelation, to tear the veil. Nor will he shrink from his self-imposed labour, Herculean though it be.

The conspiracy begins in the very Palace of the Sovereign Lady of our Ocean Isle. Leal and loyal as it is the proud vaunt of the Bleater's readers, one and all, to be, the inhabitant who pens this exposure does not personally impeach, either her Majesty the queen, or the illustrious Prince Consort. But, some silken-clad smoothers, some purple parasites, some fawners in frippery, some greedy and begartered ones in gorgeous garments, he does impeach--ay, and wrathfully! Is it asked on what grounds? They shall be stated.

The Bleater's London Correspondent, in the prosecution of his important inquiries, goes down to Windsor, sends in his card, has a confidential interview with her Majesty and the illustrious Prince Consort. For a time, the restraints of Royalty are thrown aside in the cheerful conversation of the Bleater's London Correspondent, in his fund of information, in his flow of anecdote, in the atmosphere of his genius; her Majesty brightens, the illustrious Prince Consort thaws, the cares of State and the conflicts of Party are forgotten, lunch is proposed. Over that unassuming and domestic table, her Majesty communicates to the Bleater's London Correspondent that it is her intention to send his Royal Highness the Prince of Wales to inspect the top of the Great Pyramid--thinking it likely to improve his acquaintance with the views of the people. Her Majesty further communicates that she has made up her royal mind (and that the Prince Consort has made up his illustrious mind) to the bestowal of the vacant Garter, let us say on Mr. Roebuck. The younger Royal children having been introduced at the request of the Bleater's London Correspondent, and having been by him closely observed to present the usual external indications of good health, the happy knot is severed, with a sigh the Royal bow is once more strung to its full tension, the Bleater's London Correspondent returns to London, writes his letter, and tells the Tattlesnivel Bleater what he knows. All Tattlesnivel reads it, and knows that he knows it. But, DOES his Royal Highness the Prince of Wales ultimately go to the top of the Great Pyramid? DOES Mr. Roebuck ultimately get the Garter? No. Are the younger Royal children even ultimately found to be well? On the contrary, they have--and on that very day had-- the measles. Why is this? BECAUSE THE CONSPIRATORS AGAINST THE BLEATER'S LONDON CORRESPONDENT HAVE STEPPED IN WITH THEIR DARK MACHINATIONS. Because her Majesty and the Prince Consort are artfully induced to change their minds, from north to south, from east to west, immediately after it is known to the conspirators that they have put themselves in communication with the Bleater's London Correspondent. It is now indignantly demanded, by whom are they so tampered with? It is now indignantly demanded, who took the responsibility of concealing the indisposition of those Royal children from their Royal and illustrious parents, and of bringing them down from their beds, disguised, expressly to confound the London Correspondent of the Tattlesnivel Bleater? Who are those persons, it is again asked? Let not rank and favour protect them. Let the traitors be exhibited in the face of day!

Lord John Russell is in this conspiracy. Tell us not that his Lordship is a man of too much spirit and honour. Denunciation is hurled against him. The proof? The proof is here.

The Time is panting for an answer to the question, Will Lord John Russell consent to take office under Lord Palmerston? Good. The London Correspondent of the Tattlesnivel Bleater is in the act of writing his weekly letter, finds himself rather at a loss to settle this question finally, leaves off, puts his hat on, goes down to the lobby of the House of Commons, sends in for Lord John Russell, and has him out. He draws his arm through his Lordship's, takes him aside, and says, "John, will you ever accept office under Palmerston?" His Lordship replies, "I will not." The Bleater's London Correspondent retorts, with the caution such a man is bound to use, "John, think again; say nothing to me rashly; is there any temper here?" His

Lordship replies, calmly, "None whatever." After giving him time for reflection, the Bleater's London Correspondent says, "Once more, John, let me put a question to you. Will you ever accept office under Palmerston?" His Lordship answers (note the exact expressions), "Nothing shall induce me, ever to accept a seat in a Cabinet of which Palmerston is the Chief." They part, the London Correspondent of the Tattlesnivel Bleater finishes his letter, and--always being withheld by motives of delicacy, from plainly divulging his means of getting accurate information on every subject, at first hand--puts in it, this passage: "Lord John Russell is spoken of, by blunderers, for Foreign Affairs; but I have the best reasons for assuring your readers, that" (giving prominence to the exact expressions, it will be observed) "'NOTHING WILL EVER INDUCE HIM, TO ACCEPT A SEAT IN A CABINET OF WHICH PALMERSTON IS THE CHIEF.' On this you may implicitly rely." What happens? On the very day of the publication of that number of the Bleater--the malignity of the conspirators being even manifested in the selection of the day--Lord John Russell takes the Foreign Office! Comment were superfluous.

The people of Tattlesnivel will be told, have been told, that Lord John Russell is a man of his word. He may be, on some occasions; but, when overshadowed by this dark and enormous growth of conspiracy, Tattlesnivel knows him to be otherwise. "I happen to be certain, deriving my information from a source which cannot be doubted to be authentic," wrote the London Correspondent of the Bleater, within the last year, "that Lord John Russell bitterly regrets having made that explicit speech of last Monday." These are not roundabout phrases; these are plain words. What does Lord John Russell (apparently by accident), within eight-and-forty hours after their diffusion over the civilised globe? Rises in his place in Parliament, and unblushingly declares that if the occasion could arise five hundred times, for his making that very speech, he would make it five hundred times! Is there no conspiracy here? And is this combination against one who would be always right if he were not proved always wrong, to be endured in a country that boasts of its freedom and its fairness?

But, the Tattlesnivellian who now raises his voice against intolerable oppression, may be told that, after all, this is a political conspiracy. He may be told, forsooth, that Mr. Disraeli's being in it, that Lord Derby's being in it, that Mr. Bright's being in it, that every Home, Foreign, and Colonial Secretary's being in it, that every ministry's and every opposition's being in it, are but proofs that men will do in politics what they would do in nothing else. Is this the plea? If so, the rejoinder is, that the mighty conspiracy includes the whole circle of Artists of all kinds, and comprehends all degrees of men, down to the worst criminal and the hangman who ends his career. For, all these are intimately known to the London Correspondent of the Tattlesnivel Bleater, and all these deceive him.

Sir, put it to the proof. There is the Bleater on the file-- documentary evidence. Weeks, months, before the Exhibition of the Royal Academy, the Bleater's London Correspondent knows the subjects of all the leading pictures, knows what the painters first meant to do, knows what they afterwards substituted for what they first meant to do, knows what they ought to do and won't do, knows what they ought not to do and will do, knows to a letter from whom they have commissions, knows to a shilling how much they are to be paid. Now, no sooner is each studio clear of the remarkable man to whom each studio-occupant has revealed himself as he does not reveal himself to his nearest and dearest bosom friend, than conspiracy and fraud begin. Alfred the Great becomes the Fairy Queen; Moses viewing the Promised Land, turns out to be Moses going to the Fair; Portrait of His Grace the Archbishop of Canterbury, is transformed, as if by irreverent enchantment of the dissenting interest, into A Favourite Terrier, or Cattle Grazing; and the most extraordinary work of art in the list described by the Bleater, is coolly sponged out altogether, and asserted never to have had existence at all, even in the most shadow thoughts of its executant! This is vile enough, but this is not all. Picture-buyers then come forth from their secret positions, and creep into their places in the assassin-multitude of conspirators. Mr. Baring, after expressly telling the Bleater's London Correspondent that he had bought No. 39 for one thousand guineas, gives it up to somebody unknown for a couple of hundred pounds; the Marquis of Lansdowne pretends to have no knowledge whatever of the commissions to which the London Correspondent of the Bleater swore him, but allows a Railway Contractor to cut him out for half the money. Similar examples might be multiplied. Shame, shame, on these men! Is this England?

Sir, look again at Literature. The Bleater's London Correspondent is not merely acquainted with all the eminent writers, but is in possession of the secrets of their souls. He is versed in their hidden meanings and references, sees their manuscripts before publication, and knows the subjects and titles of their books when they are not begun. How dare those writers turn upon the eminent man and depart from every intention they have confided to him? How do they justify themselves in entirely altering their manuscripts, changing their titles, and abandoning their subjects? Will they deny, in the face of Tattlesnivel, that they do so? If they have such hardihood, let the file of the Bleater strike them dumb. By their fruits they shall be known. Let their works be compared with the anticipatory letters of the Bleater's London Correspondent, and their falsehood and deceit will become manifest as the sun; it will be seen that they do nothing which they stand pledged to the Bleater's London Correspondent to do; it will be seen that they are among the blackest parties in this black and base conspiracy. This will become apparent, sir, not only as to their public proceedings but as to their private affairs. The outraged Tattlesnivellian who now drags this infamous combination into the face of day, charges those literary persons with making away with their property, imposing on the Income Tax Commissioners, keeping false books, and entering into sham contracts. He accuses them on the unimpeachable faith of the London Correspondent of the Tattlesnivel Bleater. With whose evidence they will find it impossible to reconcile their own account of any transaction of their lives.

The national character is degenerating under the influence of the ramifications of this tremendous conspiracy. Forgery is committed, constantly. A person of note--any sort of person of note--dies. The Bleater's London Correspondent knows what his circumstances are, what his savings are (if any), who his creditors are, all about his children and relations, and (in general, before his body is cold) describes his will. Is that will ever proved? Never! Some other will is substituted; the real instrument, destroyed. And this (as has been before observed), is England.

Who are the workmen and artificers, enrolled upon the books of this treacherous league? From what funds are they paid, and with what ceremonies are they sworn to secrecy? Are there none such? Observe what follows. A little time ago the Bleater's London Correspondent had this passage: "Boddleboy is pianoforte playing at St. Januarius's Gallery, with pretty tolerable success! He clears three hundred pounds per night. Not bad this!!" The builder of St. Januarius's Gallery (plunged to the throat in the conspiracy) met with this piece of news, and observed, with characteristic coarseness, "that the Bleater's London Correspondent was a Blind Ass".

Being pressed by a man of spirit to give his reasons for this extraordinary statement, he declared that the Gallery, crammed to suffocation, would not hold two hundred pounds, and that its expenses were, probably, at least half what it did hold. The man of spirit (himself a Tattlesnivellian) had the Gallery measured within a week from that hour, and it would not hold two hundred pounds! Now, can the poorest capacity doubt that it had been altered in the meantime?

And so the conspiracy extends, through every grade of society, down to the condemned criminal in prison, the hangman, and the Ordinary. Every famous murderer within the last ten years has desecrated his last moments by falsifying his confidences imparted specially to the London Correspondent of the Tattlesnivel Bleater; on every such occasion, Mr. Calcraft has followed the degrading example; and the reverend Ordinary, forgetful of his cloth, and mindful only (it would seem, alas!) of the conspiracy, has committed himself to some account or other of the criminal's demeanour and conversation, which has been diametrically opposed to the exclusive information of the London Correspondent of the Bleater. And this (as has been before observed) is Merry England!

A man of true genius, however, is not easily defeated. The Bleater's London Correspondent, probably beginning to suspect the existence of a plot against him, has recently fallen on a new style, which, as being very difficult to countermine, may necessitate the organisation of a new conspiracy. One of his masterly letters, lately, disclosed the adoption of this style--which was remarked with profound sensation throughout Tattlesnivel--in the following passage: "Mentioning literary small talk, I may tell you that some new and extraordinary rumours are afloat concerning the conversations I have previously mentioned, alleged to have taken place in the first floor front (situated over the street door), of Mr. X. Ameter (the poet so well known to your readers), in which, X. Ameter's great uncle, his second son, his butcher, and a corpulent gentleman with one eye universally respected at Kensington, are said not to have been on the most friendly footing; I forbear, however, to pursue the subject further, this week, my informant not being able to supply me with exact particulars."

But, enough, sir. The inhabitant of Tattlesnivel who has taken pen in hand to expose this odious association of unprincipled men against a shining (local) character, turns from it with disgust and contempt. Let him in few words strip the remaining flimsy covering from the nude object of the conspirators, and his loathsome task is ended.

Sir, that object, he contends, is evidently twofold. First, to exhibit the London Correspondent of the Tattlesnivel Bleater in the light of a mischievous Blockhead who, by hiring himself out to tell what he cannot possibly know, is as great a public nuisance as a Blockhead in a corner can be. Second, to suggest to the men of Tattlesnivel that it does not improve their town to have so much Dry Rubbish shot there.

Now, sir, on both these points Tattlesnivel demands in accents of Thunder, Where is the Attorney General? Why doesn't the Times take it up? (Is the latter in the conspiracy? It never adopts his views, or quotes him, and incessantly contradicts him.) Tattlesnivel, sir, remembering that our forefathers contended with the Norman at Hastings, and bled at a variety of other places that will readily occur to you, demands that its birthright shall not be bartered away for a mess of pottage. Have a care, sir, have a care! Or Tattlesnivel (its idle Rifles piled in its scouted streets) may be seen ere long, advancing with its Bleater to the foot of the Throne, and demanding redress for this conspiracy, from the orbed and sceptred hands of Majesty itself!

THE YOUNG MAN FROM THE COUNTRY

A song of the hour, now in course of being sung and whistled in every street, the other day reminded the writer of these words--as he chanced to pass a fag-end of the song for the twentieth time in a short London walk--that twenty years ago, a little book on the United States, entitled American Notes, was published by "a Young Man from the Country", who had just seen and left it.

This Young Man from the Country fell into a deal of trouble, by reason of having taken the liberty to believe that he perceived in America downward popular tendencies for which his young enthusiasm had been anything but prepared. It was in vain for the Young Man to offer in extenuation of his belief that no stranger could have set foot on those shores with a feeling of livelier interest in the country, and stronger faith in it, than he. Those were the days when the Tories had made their Ashburton Treaty, and when Whigs and Radicals must have no theory disturbed. All three parties waylaid and mauled the Young Man from the Country, and showed that he knew nothing about the country.

As the Young Man from the Country had observed in the Preface to his little book, that he "could bide his time", he took all this in silent part for eight years. Publishing then, a cheap edition of his book, he made no stronger protest than the following:

"My readers have opportunities of judging for themselves whether the influences and tendencies which I distrusted in America, have any existence but in my imagination. They can examine for themselves whether there has been anything in the public career of that country during these past eight years, or whether there is anything in its present position, at home or abroad, which suggests that those influences and tendencies really do exist. As they find the fact, they will judge me. If they discern any evidences of wrong-going, in any direction that I have indicated, they will acknowledge that I had reason in what I wrote. If they discern no such thing, they will consider me altogether mistaken. I have nothing to defend, or to explain away. The truth is the truth; and neither childish absurdities, nor unscrupulous contradictions, can make it otherwise. The earth would still move round the sun, though the whole Catholic Church said No."

Twelve more years having since passed away, it may now, at last, be simply just towards the Young Man from the Country, to compare what he originally wrote, with recent events and their plain motive powers. Treating of the House of Representatives at Washington, he wrote thus:

"Did I recognise in this assembly, a body of men, who, applying themselves in a new world to correct some of the falsehoods and vices of the old, purified the avenues to Public Life, paved the dirty ways to Place and Power, debated and made laws for the Common Good, and had no party but their Country?

"I saw in them, the wheels that move the meanest perversion of virtuous Political Machinery that the worst tools ever wrought. Despicable trickery at elections; under-handed tamperings with public officers; cowardly attacks upon opponents, with scurrilous newspapers for shields, and hired pens for daggers; shameful trucklings to mercenary knaves, whose claim to be considered, is, that every day and week they sow new crops of ruin with their venal types, which are the dragon's teeth of yore, in everything but sharpness; aidings and abettings of every bad inclination in the popular mind, and artful suppressions of all its good influences: such things as these, and in a word, Dishonest Faction in its most depraved and most unblushing form, stared out from every corner of the crowded hall.

"Did I see among them, the intelligence and refinement: the true, honest, patriotic heart of America? Here and there, were drops of its blood and life, but they scarcely coloured the stream of desperate adventurers which sets that way for profit and for pay. It is the game of these men, and of their profligate organs, to make the strife of politics so fierce and brutal, and so destructive of all self-respect in worthy men, that sensitive and delicate-minded persons shall be kept aloof, and they, and such as they, be left to battle out their selfish views unchecked. And thus this lowest of all scrambling fights goes on, and they who in other countries would, from their intelligence and station, most aspire to make the laws, do here recoil the farthest from that degradation.

"That there are, among the representatives of the people in both Houses, and among all parties, some men of high character and great abilities, I need not say. The foremost among those politicians who are known in Europe, have been already described, and I see no reason to depart from the rule I have laid down for my guidance, of abstaining from all mention of individuals. It will be sufficient to add, that to the most favourable accounts that have been written of them, I fully and most heartily subscribe; and that personal intercourse and free communication have bred within me, not the result predicted in the very doubtful proverb, but increased admiration and respect."

Towards the end of his book, the Young Man from the Country thus expressed himself concerning its people:

"They are, by nature, frank, brave, cordial, hospitable, and affectionate. Cultivation and refinement seem but to enhance their warmth of heart and ardent enthusiasm; and it is the possession of these latter qualities in a most remarkable degree, which renders an educated American one of the most endearing and most generous of friends. I never was so won upon, as by this class; never yielded up my full confidence and esteem so readily and pleasurably, as to them; never can make again, in half a year, so many friends for whom I seem to entertain the regard of half a life.

"These qualities are natural, I implicitly believe, to the whole people. That they are, however, sadly sapped and blighted in their growth among the mass; and that there are influences at work which endanger them still more, and give but little present promise of their healthy restoration; is a truth that ought to be told.

"It is an essential part of every national character to pique itself mightily upon its faults, and to deduce tokens of its virtue or its wisdom from their very exaggeration. One great blemish in the popular mind of America, and the prolific parent of an innumerable brood of evils, is Universal Distrust. Yet the American citizen plumes himself upon this spirit, even when he is sufficiently dispassionate to perceive the ruin it works; and will often adduce it, in spite of his own reason, as an instance of the great sagacity and acuteness of the people, and their superior shrewdness and independence.

"'You carry,' says the stranger, 'this jealousy and distrust into every transaction of public life. By repelling worthy men from your legislative assemblies, it has bred up a class of candidates for the suffrage, who, in their every act, disgrace your Institutions and your people's choice. It has rendered you so fickle, and so given to change, that your inconstancy has passed into a proverb; for you no sooner set up an idol firmly, than you are sure to pull it down and dash it into fragments: and this, because directly you reward a benefactor, or a public-servant, you distrust him, merely because he IS rewarded; and immediately apply yourselves to find out, either that you have been too bountiful in your acknowledgments, or he remiss in his deserts. Any man who attains a high place among you, from the President downwards, may date his downfall from that moment; for any printed lie that any notorious villain pens, although it militate directly against the character and conduct of a life, appeals at once to your distrust, and is believed. You will strain at a gnat in the way of trustfulness and confidence, however fairly won and well deserved; but you will swallow a whole caravan of camels, if they be laden with unworthy doubts and mean suspicions. Is this well, think you, or likely to elevate the character of the governors or the governed, among you?'

"The answer is invariably the same: 'There's freedom of opinion here, you know. Every man thinks for himself, and we are not to be easily overreached. That's how our people come to be suspicious.'

"Another prominent feature is the love of 'smart' dealing: which gilds over many a swindle and gross breach of trust; many a defalcation, public and private; and enables many a knave to hold his head up with the best, who well deserves a halter: though it has not been without its retributive operation, for this smartness has done more in a few years to impair the public credit, and to cripple the public resources, than dull honesty, however rash, could have effected in a century. The merits of a broken speculation, or a bankruptcy, or of a successful scoundrel, are not gauged by its or his observance of the golden rule, 'Do as you would be done by', but are considered with reference to their smartness. I recollect, on both occasions of our passing that ill-fated Cairo on the Mississippi, remarking on the bad effects such gross deceits must have when they exploded, in generating a want of confidence abroad, and discouraging foreign investment: but I was given to understand that this was a very smart scheme by which a deal of money had been made: and that its smartest feature was, that they forgot these things abroad, in a very short time, and speculated again, as freely as ever. The following dialogue I have held a hundred times: 'Is it not a very disgraceful circumstance that such a man as So-and-so should be acquiring a large property by the most infamous and odious means, and notwithstanding all the crimes of which he has been guilty, should be tolerated and abetted by your citizens? He is a public nuisance, is he not?' 'Yes, sir.' 'A convicted liar?' 'Yes, sir.' 'He has been kicked, and cuffed, and caned?' 'Yes, sir.' 'And he is utterly dishonourable, debased, and profligate?' 'Yes, sir.' 'In the name of wonder, then, what is his merit?' 'Well, sir, he is a smart man.'

"But the foul growth of America has a more tangled root than this; and it strikes its fibres, deep in its licentious Press.

"Schools may he erected, East, West, North, and South; pupils be taught, and masters reared, by scores upon scores of thousands; colleges may thrive, churches may be crammed, temperance may be diffused, and advancing knowledge in all other forms walk through the land with giant strides; but while the newspaper press of America is in, or near, its present abject state, high moral improvement in that country is hopeless. Year by year, it must and will go back; year by year, the tone of public opinion must sink lower down; year by year, the Congress and the Senate must become of less account before all decent men; and year by year, the memory of the Great Fathers of the Revolution must be outraged more and more, in the bad life of their degenerate child.

"Among the herd of journals which are published in the States, there are some, the reader scarcely need be told, of character and credit. From personal intercourse with accomplished gentlemen connected with publications of this class, I have derived both pleasure and profit. But the name of these is Few, and of the others Legion; and the influence of the good, is powerless to counteract the moral poison of the bad.

"Among the gentry of America; among the well-informed and moderate; in the learned professions; at the bar and on the bench; there is, as there can be, but one opinion, in reference to the vicious character of these infamous journals. It is sometimes contended--I will not say strangely, for it is natural to seek excuses for such a disgrace--that their influence is not so great as a visitor would suppose. I must be pardoned for saying that there is no warrant for this plea, and that every fact and circumstance tends directly to the opposite conclusion.

"When any man, of any grade of desert in intellect or character, can climb to any public distinction, no matter what, in America, without first grovelling down upon the earth, and bending the knee before this monster of depravity; when any private excellence is safe from its attacks; when any social confidence is left unbroken by it; or any tie of social decency and honour is held in the least regard; when any man in that Free Country has freedom of opinion, and presumes to think for himself, and speak for himself, without humble reference to a censorship which, for its rampant ignorance and base dishonesty, he utterly loaths and despises in his heart; when those who most acutely feel its infamy and the reproach it casts upon the nation, and who most denounce it to each other, dare to set their heels upon, and crush it openly, in the sight of all men: then, I will believe that its influence is lessening, and men are returning to their manly senses. But while that Press has its evil eye in every house, and its black hand in every appointment in the state, from a president to a postman; while, with ribald slander for its only stock in trade, it is the standard literature of an enormous class, who must find their reading in a newspaper, or they will not read at all; so long must its odium be upon the country's head, and so long must the evil it works, be plainly visible in the Republic."

The foregoing was written in the year eighteen hundred and forty- two. It rests with the reader to decide whether it has received any confirmation, or assumed any colour of truth, in or about the year eighteen hundred and sixty-two.

AN ENLIGHTENED CLERGYMAN

At various places in Suffolk (as elsewhere) penny readings take place "for the instruction and amusement of the lower classes". There is a little town in Suffolk called Eye, where the subject of one of these readings was a tale (by Mr. Wilkie Collins) from the last Christmas Number of this Journal, entitled "Picking up Waifs at Sea". It appears that the Eye gentility was shocked by the introduction of this rude piece among the taste and musical glasses of that important town, on which the eyes of Europe are notoriously always fixed. In particular, the feelings of the vicar's family were outraged; and a Local Organ (say, the Tattlesnivel Bleater) consequently doomed the said piece to everlasting oblivion, as being of an "injurious tendency!"

When this fearful fact came to the knowledge of the unhappy writer of the doomed tale in question, he covered his face with his robe, previous to dying decently under the sharp steel of the ecclesiastical gentility of the terrible town of Eye. But the discovery that he was not alone in his gloomy glory, revived him, and he still lives.

For, at Stowmarket, in the aforesaid county of Suffolk, at another of those penny readings, it was announced that a certain juvenile sketch, culled from a volume of sketches (by Boz) and entitled "The Bloomsbury Christening", would be read. Hereupon, the clergyman of that place took heart and pen, and addressed the following terrific epistle to a gentleman bearing the very appropriate name of Gudgeon:

STOWMARKET VICARAGE, Feb. 25, 1861.

SIR,--My attention has been directed to a piece called "The Bloomsbury Christening" which you propose to read this evening. Without presuming to claim any interference in the arrangement of the readings, I would suggest to you whether you have on this occasion sufficiently considered the character of the composition you have selected. I quite appreciate the laudable motive of the promoters of the readings to raise the moral tone amongst the working class of the town and to direct this taste in a familiar and pleasant manner. "The Bloomsbury Christening" cannot possibly do this. It trifles with a sacred ordinance, and the language and style, instead of improving the taste, has a direct tendency to lower it.

I appeal to your right feeling whether it is desirable to give publicity to that which must shock several of your audience, and create a smile amongst others, to be indulged in only by violating the conscientious scruples of their neighbours.

The ordinance which is here exposed to ridicule is one which is much misunderstood and neglected amongst many families belonging to the Church of England, and the mode in which it is treated in this chapter cannot fail to appear as giving a sanction to, or at least excusing, such neglect.

Although you are pledged to the public to give this subject, yet I cannot but believe that they would fully justify your substitution of it for another did they know the circumstances. An abridgment would only lessen the evil in a degree, as it is not only the style of the writing but the subject itself which is objectionable.

Excuse me for troubling you, but I felt that, in common with yourself, I have a grave responsibility in the matter, and I am most truly yours,

T. S. COLES. To Mr. J. Gudgeon.

It is really necessary to explain that this is not a bad joke. It is simply a bad fact.

RATHER A STRONG DOSE

Doctor John Campbell, the minister of the Tabernacle Chapel, Finsbury, and editor of the British Banner, etc., with that massive vigour which distinguishes his style," did, we are informed by Mr. Howitt, "deliver a verdict in the Banner, for November, 1852," of great importance and favour to the Table-rapping cause. We are not informed whether the Public, sitting in judgment on the question, reserved any point in this great verdict for subsequent consideration; but the verdict would seem to have been regarded by a perverse generation as not quite final, inasmuch as Mr. Howitt finds it necessary to re-open the case, a round ten years afterwards, in nine hundred and sixty-two stiff octavo pages, published by Messrs. Longman and Company.

Mr. Howitt is in such a bristling temper on the Supernatural subject, that we will not take the great liberty of arguing any point with him. But--with the view of assisting him to make converts--we will inform our readers, on his conclusive authority, what they are required to believe; premising what may rather astonish them in connexion with their views of a certain historical trifle, called The Reformation, that their present state of unbelief is all the fault of Protestantism, and that "it is high time, therefore, to protest against Protestantism".

They will please to believe, by way of an easy beginning, all the stories of good and evil demons, ghosts, prophecies, communication with spirits, and practice of magic, that ever obtained, or are said to have ever obtained, in the North, in the South, in the East, in the West, from the earliest and darkest ages, as to which we have any hazy intelligence, real or supposititious, down to the yet unfinished displacement of the red men in North America. They will please to believe that nothing in this wise was changed by the fulfilment of our Saviour's mission upon earth; and further, that what Saint Paul did, can be done again, and has been done again. As this is not much to begin with, they will throw in at this point rejection of Faraday and Brewster, and "poor Paley", and implicit acceptance of those shining lights, the Reverend Charles Beecher, and the Reverend Henry Ward Beecher ("one of the most vigorous and eloquent preachers of America"), and the Reverend Adin Ballou.

Having thus cleared the way for a healthy exercise of faith, our advancing readers will next proceed especially to believe in the old story of the Drummer of Tedworth, in the inspiration of George Fox, in "the spiritualism, prophecies, and provision" of Huntington the coal-porter (him who prayed for the leather breeches which miraculously fitted him), and even in the Cock Lane Ghost. They will please wind up, before fetching their breath, with believing that there is a close analogy between rejection of any such plain and proved facts as those contained in the whole foregoing catalogue, and the opposition encountered by the inventors of railways, lighting by gas, microscopes and telescopes, and vaccination. This stinging consideration they will always carry rankling in their remorseful hearts as they advance.

As touching the Cock Lane Ghost, our conscience-stricken readers will please particularly to reproach themselves for having ever supposed that important spiritual manifestation to have been a gross imposture which was thoroughly detected. They will please to believe that Dr. Johnson believed in it, and that, in Mr. Howitt's words, he "appears to have had excellent reasons for his belief". With a view to this end, the faithful will be so good as to obliterate from their Boswells the following passage: "Many of my readers, I am convinced, are to this hour under an impression that Johnson was thus foolishly deceived. It will therefore surprise them a good deal when they are informed upon undoubted authority that Johnson was one of those by whom the imposture was detected. The story had become so popular, that he thought it should be investigated, and in this research he was assisted by the Rev. Dr. Douglas, now Bishop of Salisbury, the great detector of impostures"- -and therefore tremendously obnoxious to Mr. Howitt--"who informs me that after the gentlemen who went and examined into the evidence were satisfied of its falsity, Johnson wrote in their presence an account of it, which was published in the newspapers and Gentleman's Magazine, and undeceived the world". But as there will still remain another highly inconvenient passage in the Boswells of the true believers, they must likewise be at the trouble of cancelling the following also, referring to a later time: "He (Johnson) expressed great indignation at the imposture of the Cock Lane Ghost, and related with much satisfaction how he had assisted in detecting the cheat, and had published an account of it in the newspapers".

They will next believe (if they be, in the words of Captain Bobadil, "so generously minded") in the transatlantic trance-speakers "who professed to speak from direct inspiration", Mrs. Cora Hatch, Mrs. Henderson, and Miss Emma Hardinge; and they will believe in those eminent ladies having "spoken on Sundays to five hundred thousand hearers"--small audiences, by the way, compared with the intelligent concourse recently assembled in the city of New York, to do honour to the Nuptials of General the Honourable T. Barnum Thumb. At about this stage of their spiritual education they may take the opportunity of believing in "letters from a distinguished gentleman of New York, in which the frequent appearance of the gentleman's deceased wife and of Dr. Franklin, to him and other well-known friends, are unquestionably unequalled in the annals of the marvellous". Why these modest appearances should seem at all out of the common way to Mr. Howitt (who would be in a state of flaming indignation if we thought them so), we could not imagine, until we found on reading further, "it is solemnly stated that the witnesses have not only seen but touched these spirits, and handled the clothes and hair of Franklin". Without presuming to go Mr. Howitt's length of considering this by any means a marvellous experience, we yet venture to confess that it has awakened in our mind many interesting speculations touching the present whereabout in space, of the spirits of Mr. Howitt's own departed boots and hats.

The next articles of belief are Belief in the moderate figures of "thirty thousand media in the United States in 1853"; and in two million five hundred thousand spiritualists in the same country of composed minds, in 1855, "professing to have arrived at their convictions of spiritual communication from personal experience"; and in "an average rate of increase of three hundred thousand per annum", still in the same country of calm philosophers. Belief in spiritual knockings, in all manner of American places, and, among others, in the house of "a Doctor Phelps at Stratford, Connecticut, a man of the highest character for intelligence", says Mr. Howitt, and to whom we willingly concede the possession of far higher intelligence than was displayed by his spiritual knocker, in "frequently cutting to pieces the clothes of one of his boys", and in breaking "seventy-one panes of glass"--unless, indeed, the knocker, when in the body, was connected with the tailoring and glazing interests. Belief in immaterial performers playing (in the dark though: they are obstinate about its being in the dark) on material instruments of wood, catgut, brass, tin, and parchment. Your belief is further requested in "the Kentucky Jerks". The spiritual achievements thus euphoniously denominated "appear", says Mr. Howitt, "to have been of a very disorderly kind". It appears that a certain Mr. Doke, a Presbyterian clergyman, "was first seized by the jerks", and the jerks laid hold of Mr. Doke in that unclerical way and with that scant respect for his cloth, that they "twitched him about in a most extraordinary manner, often when in the pulpit, and caused him to shout aloud, and run out of the pulpit into the woods, screaming like a madman. When the fit was over, he returned calmly to his pulpit and finished the service." The congregation having waited, we presume, and edified themselves with the distant bellowings of Doke in the woods, until he came back again, a little warm and hoarse, but otherwise in fine condition. "People were often seized at hotels, and at table would, on lifting a glass to drink, jerk the liquor to the ceiling; ladies would at the breakfast-table suddenly be compelled to throw aloft their coffee, and frequently break the cup and saucer." A certain venturesome clergyman vowed that he would preach down the Jerks, "but he was seized in the midst of his attempt, and made so ridiculous that he withdrew himself from further notice"--an example much to be commended. That same favoured land of America has been particularly favoured in the development of "innumerable mediums", and Mr. Howitt orders you to believe in Daniel Dunglas Home, Andrew Davis Jackson, and Thomas L. Harris, as "the three most remarkable, or most familiar, on this side of the Atlantic". Concerning Mr. Home, the articles of belief (besides removal of furniture) are, That through him raps have been given and communications made from deceased friends. That "his hand has been seized by spirit influence, and rapid communications written out, of a surprising character to those to whom they were addressed". That at his bidding, "spirit hands have appeared which have been seen, felt, and recognised frequently, by persons present, as those of deceased friends". That he has been frequently lifted up and carried, floating "as it were" through a room, near the ceiling. That in America, "all these phenomena have displayed themselves in greater force than here"--which we have not the slightest doubt of.

That he is "the planter of spiritualism all over Europe". That "by circumstances that no man could have devised, he became the guest of the Emperor of the French, of the King of Holland, of the Czar of Russia, and of many lesser princes". That he returned from "this unpremeditated missionary tour", "endowed with competence"; but not before, "at the Tuileries, on one occasion when the emperor, empress, a distinguished lady, and himself only were sitting at table, a hand appeared, took up a pen, and wrote, in a strong and well-known character, the word Napoleon. The hand was then successively presented to the several personages of the party to kiss." The stout believer, having disposed of Mr. Home, and rested a little, will then proceed to believe in Andrew Davis Jackson, or Andrew Jackson Davis (Mr. Howitt, having no Medium at hand to settle this difference and reveal the right name of the seer, calls him by both names), who merely "beheld all the essential natures of things, saw the interior of men and animals, as perfectly as their exterior; and described them in language so correct, that the most able technologists could not surpass him. He pointed out the proper remedies for all the complaints, and the shops where they were to be obtained";--in the latter respect appearing to hail from an advertising circle, as we conceive. It was also in this gentleman's limited department to "see the metals in the earth", and to have "the most distant regions and their various productions present before him". Having despatched this tough case, the believer will pass on to Thomas L. Harris, and will swallow HIM easily, together with "whole epics" of his composition; a certain work "of scarcely less than Miltonic grandeur", called The Lyric of the Golden Age--a lyric pretty nigh as long as one of Mr. Howitt's volumes--dictated by Mr. (not Mrs.) Harris to the publisher in ninety-four hours; and several extempore sermons, possessing the remarkably lucid property of being "full, unforced, out-gushing, unstinted, and absorbing". The candidate for examination in pure belief, will then pass on to the spirit-photography department; this, again, will be found in so- favoured America, under the superintendence of Medium Mumler, a photographer of Boston: who was "astonished" (though, on Mr. Howitt's showing, he surely ought not to have been) "on taking a photograph of himself, to find also by his side the figure of a young girl, which he immediately recognised as that of a deceased relative. The circumstance made a great excitement. Numbers of persons rushed to his rooms, and many have found deceased friends photographed with themselves." (Perhaps Mr. Mumler, too, may become "endowed with competence" in time. Who knows?) Finally, the true believers in the gospel according to Howitt, have, besides, but to pin their faith on "ladies who see spirits habitually", on ladies who KNOW they have a tendency to soar in the air on sufficient provocation, and on a few other gnats to be taken after their camels, and they shall be pronounced by Mr. Howitt not of the stereotyped class of minds, and not partakers of "the astonishing ignorance of the press", and shall receive a first-class certificate of merit.

But before they pass through this portal into the Temple of Serene Wisdom, we, halting blind and helpless on the steps, beg to suggest to them what they must at once and for ever disbelieve. They must disbelieve that in the dark times, when very few were versed in what are now the mere recreations of Science, and when those few formed a priesthood-class apart, any marvels were wrought by the aid of concave mirrors and a knowledge of the properties of certain odours and gases, although the self-same marvels could be reproduced before their eyes at the Poly-technic Institution, Regent Street, London, any day in the year. They must by no means believe that Conjuring and Ventriloquism are old trades. They must disbe-lieve all Philosophical Transactions containing the records of painful and careful inquiry into now familiar disorders of the senses of seeing and hearing, and into the wonders of somnambulism, epilepsy, hysteria, miasmatic influence, vegetable poisons derived by whole communities from corrupted air, diseased imitation, and moral infection. They must disbelieve all such awkward leading cases as the case of the Woodstock Commissioners and their man, and the case of the Identity of the Stockwell Ghost, with the maid-servant. They must disbelieve the vanishing of champion haunted houses (except, indeed, out of Mr. Howitt's book), represented to have been closed and ruined for years, before one day's inquiry by four gentle-men associated with this journal, and one hour's reference to the Local Rate-books. They must disbelieve all possibility of a human creature on the last verge of the dark bridge from Life to Death, being mysteriously able, in occasional cases, so to influence the mind of one very near and dear, as vividly to impress that mind with some disturbed sense of the solemn change impending. They must disbelieve the possibility of the lawful existence of a class of intellects which, humbly conscious of the illimitable power of GOD and of their own weakness and ignorance, never deny that He can cause the souls of the dead to revisit the earth, or that He may have caused the souls of the dead to revisit the earth, or that He can cause any awful or wondrous thing to be; but to deny the likelihood of apparitions or spirits coming here upon the stupidest of bootless errands, and producing credentials tantamount to a solicitation of our vote and interest and next proxy, to get them into the Asylum for Idiots. They must disbelieve the right of Christian people who do NOT protest against Protestantism, but who hold it to be a barrier against the darkest superstitions that can enslave the soul, to guard with jealousy all approaches tending down to Cock Lane Ghosts and suchlike infamous swindles, widely degrading when widely believed in; and they must disbelieve that such people have the right to know, and that it is their duty to know, wonder- workers by their fruits, and to test miracle-mongers by the tests of probability, analogy, and common sense. They must disbelieve all rational explanations of thoroughly proved experiences (only) which appear supernatural, derived from the average experience and study of the visible world. They must disbelieve the speciality of the Master and the Disciples, and that it is a monstrosity to test the wonders of show-folk by the same touchstone. Lastly, they must disbelieve that one of the best accredited chapters in the history of mankind is the chapter that records the astonishing deceits continually practised, with no object or purpose but the distorted pleasure of deceiving.

We have summed up a few--not nearly all--of the articles of belief and disbelief to which Mr. Howitt most arrogantly demands an implicit adherence. To uphold these, he uses a book as a Clown in a Pantomime does, and knocks everybody on the head with it who comes in his way. Moreover, he is an angrier personage than the Clown, and does not experimentally try the effect of his red-hot poker on your shins, but straightway runs you through the body and soul with it. He is always raging to tell you that if you are not Howitt, you are Atheist and Anti-Christ. He is the sans-culotte of the Spiritual Revolution, and will not hear of your accepting this point and rejecting that;--down your throat with them all, one and indivisible, at the point of the pike; No Liberty, Totality, Fraternity, or Death!

Without presuming to question that "it is high time to protest against Protestantism" on such very substantial grounds as Mr. Howitt sets forth, we do presume to think that it is high time to protest against Mr. Howitt's spiritualism, as being a little in excess of the peculiar merit of Thomas L. Harris's sermons, and somewhat TOO "full, out-gushing, unstinted, and absorbing".

THE MARTYR MEDIUM

After the valets, the master!" is Mr. Fechter's rallying cry in the picturesque romantic drama which attracts all London to the Lyceum Theatre. After the worshippers and puffers of Mr. Daniel Dunglas Home, the spirit medium, comes Mr. Daniel Dunglas Home himself, in one volume. And we must, for the honour of Literature, plainly express our great surprise and regret that he comes arm-in-arm with such good company as Messrs. Longman and Company.

We have already summed up Mr. Home's demands on the public capacity of swallowing, as sounded through the war-denouncing trumpet of Mr. Howitt, and it is not our intention to revive the strain as performed by Mr. Home on his own melodious instrument. We notice, by the way, that in that part of the Fantasia where the hand of the first Napoleon is supposed to be reproduced, recognised, and kissed, at the Tuileries, Mr. Home subdues the florid effects one might have expected after Mr. Howitt's execution, and brays in an extremely general manner. And yet we observe Mr. Home to be in other things very reliant on Mr. Howitt, of whom he entertains as gratifying an opinion as Mr. Howitt entertains of him: dwelling on his "deep researches into this subject", and of his "great work now ready for the press", and of his "eloquent and forcible" advocacy, and eke of his "elaborate and almost exhaustive work", which Mr. Home trusts will be "extensively read". But, indeed, it would seem to be the most reliable characteristic of the Dear Spirits, though very capricious in other particulars, that they always form their circles into what may be described, in worldly terms, as A Mutual Admiration and Complimentation Company (Limited).

Mr. Home's book is entitled Incidents in My Life. We will extract a dozen sample passages from it, as variations on and phrases of harmony in, the general strain for the Trumpet, which we have promised not to repeat.

1. MR. HOME IS SUPERNATURALLY NURSED

"I cannot remember when first I became subject to the curious phenomena which have now for so long attended me, but my aunt and others have told me that when I was a baby my cradle was frequently rocked, as if some kind guardian spirit was attending me in my slumbers."

2. DISRESPECTFUL CONDUCT OF MR. HOME'S AUNT NEVERTHELESS

"In her uncontrollable anger she seized a chair and threw it at me."

3. PUNISHMENT OF MR. HOME'S AUNT

"Upon one occasion as the table was being thus moved about of itself, my aunt brought the family Bible, and placing it on the table, said, 'There, that will soon drive the devils away'; but to her astonishment the table only moved in a more lively manner, as if pleased to bear such a burden." (We believe this is constantly observed in pulpits and church reading desks, which are invariably lively.) "Seeing this she was greatly incensed, and determined to stop it, she angrily placed her whole weight on the table, and was actually lifted up with it bodily from the floor."

4. TRIUMPHANT EFFECT OF THIS DISCIPLINE ON MR. HOME'S AUNT

"And she felt it a duty that I should leave her house, and which I did."

5. MR. HOME'S MISSION

It was communicated to him by the spirit of his mother, in the following terms: "Daniel, fear not, my child, God is with you, and who shall be against you? Seek to do good: be truthful and truth- loving, and you will prosper, my child. Yours is a glorious mission--you will convince the infidel, cure the sick, and console the weeping." It is a coincidence that another eminent man, with several missions, heard a voice from the Heavens blessing him, when he also was a youth, and saying, "You will be rewarded, my son, in time". This Medium was the celebrated Baron Munchausen, who relates the experience in the opening of the second chapter of the incidents in HIS life.

6. MODEST SUCCESS OF MR. HOME'S MISSION

"Certainly these phenomena, whether from God or from the devil, have in ten years caused more converts to the great truths of immortality and angel communion, with all that flows from these great facts, than all the sects in Christendom have made during the same period."

7. WHAT THE FIRST COMPOSERS SAY OF THE SPIRIT-MUSIC, TO MR. HOME

"As to the music, it has been my good fortune to be on intimate terms with some of the first composers of the day, and more than one of them have said of such as they have heard, that it is such music as only angels could make, and no man could write it."

These "first composers" are not more particularly named. We shall therefore be happy to receive and file at the office of this Journal, the testimonials in the foregoing terms of Dr. Sterndale Bennett, Mr. Balfe, Mr. Macfarren, Mr. Benedict, Mr. Vincent Wallace, Signor Costa, M. Auber, M. Gounod, Signor Rossini, and Signor Verdi. We shall also feel obliged to Mr. Alfred Mellon, who is no doubt constantly studying this wonderful music, under the Medium's auspices, if he will note on paper, from memory, say a single sheet of the same. Signor Giulio Regondi will then perform it, as correctly as a mere mortal can, on the Accordion, at the next ensuing concert of the Philharmonic Society; on which occasion the before-mentioned testimonials will be conspicuously displayed in the front of the orchestra.

8. MR. HOME'S MIRACULOUS INFANT

"On the 26th April, old style, or 8th May, according to our style, at seven in the evening, and as the snow was fast falling, our little boy was born at the town house, situate on the Gagarines Quay, in St. Petersburg, where we were still staying. A few hours after his birth, his mother, the nurse, and I heard for several hours the warbling of a bird as if singing over him. Also that night, and for two or three nights afterwards, a bright starlike light, which was clearly visible from the partial darkness of the room, in which there was only a night-lamp burning, appeared several times directly I over its head, where it remained for some moments, and then slowly moved in the direction of the door, where it disappeared. This was also seen by each of us at the same time. The light was more condensed than those which have been so often seen in my presence upon previous and subsequent occasions. It was brighter and more distinctly globular. I do not believe that it came through my mediumship, but rather through that of the child, who has manifested on several occasions the presence of the gift. I do not like to allude to such a matter, but as there are more strange things in Heaven and earth than are dreamt of, even in my philosophy, I do not feel myself at liberty to omit stating, that during the latter part of my wife's pregnancy, we thought it better that she should not join in Seances, because it was found that whenever the rappings occurred in the room, a simultaneous movement of the child was distinctly felt, perfectly in unison with the sounds. When there were three sounds, three movements were felt, and so on, and when five sounds were heard, which is generally the call for the alphabet, she felt the five internal movements, and she would frequently, when we were mistaken in the latter, correct us from what the child indicated."

We should ask pardon of our readers for sullying our paper with this nauseous matter, if without it they could adequately understand what Mr. Home's book is.

9. CAGLIOSTRO'S SPIRIT CALLS ON MR. HOME

Prudently avoiding the disagreeable question of his giving himself, both in this state of existence and in his spiritual circle, a name to which he never had any pretensions whatever, and likewise prudently suppressing any reference to his amiable weakness as a swindler and an infamous trafficker in his own wife, the guileless Mr. Balsamo delivered, in a "distinct voice", this distinct celestial utterance--unquestionably punctuated in a supernatural manner: "My power was that of a mesmerist, but all-misunderstood by those about me, my biographers have even done me injustice, but I care not for the untruths of earth".

10. ORACULAR STATE OF MR. HOME

"After various manifestations, Mr. Home went into the trance, and addressing a person present, said, 'You ask what good are such trivial manifestations, such as rapping, table-moving, etc.? God is a better judge than we are what is fitted for humanity, immense results may spring from trivial things. The steam from a kettle is a small thing, but look at the locomotive! The electric spark from the back of a cat is a small thing, but see the wonders of electricity! The raps are small things, but their results will lead you to the Spirit-World, and to eternity! Why should great results spring from such small causes? Christ was born in a manger, he was not born a King. When you tell me why he was born in a manger, I will tell you why these manifestations, so trivial, so undignified as they appear to you, have been appointed to convince the world of the truth of spiritualism.'"

Wonderful! Clearly direct Inspiration!--And yet, perhaps, hardly worth the trouble of going "into the trance" for, either. Amazing as the revelation is, we seem to have heard something like it from more than one personage who was wide awake. A quack doctor, in an open barouche (attended by a barrel-organ and two footmen in brass helmets), delivered just such another address within our hearing, outside a gate of Paris, not two months ago.

11. THE TESTIMONY OF MR. HOME'S BOOTS

"The lady of the house turned to me and said abruptly, 'Why, you are sitting in the air'; and on looking, we found that the chair remained in its place, but that I was elevated two or three inches above it, and my feet not touching the floor. This may show how utterly unconscious I am at times to the sensation of levitation. As is usual, when I had not got above the level of the heads of those about me, and when they change their position much--as they frequently do in looking wistfully at such a phenomenon--I came down again, but not till I had remained so raised about half a minute from the time of its being first seen. I was now impressed to leave the table, and was soon carried to the lofty ceiling. The Count de B- left his place at the table, and coming under where I was, said, 'Now, young Home, come and let me touch your feet.' I told him I had no volition in the matter, but perhaps the spirits would kindly allow me to come down to him. They did so, by floating me down to him, and my feet were soon in his outstretched hands. He seized my boots, and now I was again elevated, he holding tightly, and pulling at my feet, till the boots I wore, which had elastic sides, came off and remained in his hands."

12. THE UNCOMBATIVE NATURE OF MR. HOME

As there is a maudlin complaint in this book, about men of Science being hard upon "the 'Orphan' Home", and as the "gentle and uncombative nature" of this Medium in a martyred point of view is pathetically commented on by the anonymous literary friend who supplies him with an introduction and appendix--rather at odds with Mr. Howitt, who is so mightily triumphant about the same Martyr's reception by crowned heads, and about the competence he has become endowed with--we cull from Mr. Home's book one or two little illustrative flowers. Sir David Brewster (a pestilent unbeliever) "has come before the public in few matters which have brought more shame upon him than his conduct and assertions on this occasion, in which he manifested not only a disregard for truth, but also a disloyalty to scientific observation, and to the use of his own eyesight and natural faculties". The same unhappy Sir David Brewster's "character may be the better known, not only for his untruthful dealing with this subject, but also in his own domain of science in which the same unfaithfulness to truth will be seen to be the characteristic of his mind". Again, he "is really not a man over whom victory is any honour". Again, "not only he, but Professor Faraday have had time and ample leisure to regret that they should have so foolishly pledged themselves", etc. A Faraday a fool in the sight of a Home! That unjust judge and whited wall, Lord Brougham, has his share of this Martyr Medium's uncombativeness. "In order that he might not be compelled to deny Sir David's statements, he found it necessary that he should be silent, and I have some reason to complain that his Lordship preferred sacrificing me to his desire not to immolate his friend." M. Arago also came off with very doubtful honours from a wrestle with the uncombative Martyr; who is perfectly clear (and so are we, let us add) that scientific men are not the men for his purpose. Of course, he is the butt of "utter and acknowledged ignorance", and of "the most gross and foolish statements", and of "the unjust and dishonest", and of "the press-gang", and of crowds of other alien and combative adjectives, participles, and substantives.

Nothing is without its use, and even this odious book may do some service. Not because it coolly claims for the writer and his disciples such powers as were wielded by the Saviour and the Apostles; not because it sees no difference between twelve table rappers in these days, and "twelve fishermen" in those; not because it appeals for precedents to statements extracted from the most ignorant and wretched of mankind, by cruel torture, and constantly withdrawn when the torture was withdrawn; not because it sets forth such a strange confusion of ideas as is presented by one of the faithful when, writing of a certain sprig of geranium handed by an invisible hand, he adds in ecstasies, "WHICH WE HAVE PLANTED AND IT IS GROWING, SO THAT IT IS NO DELUSION, NO FAIRY MONEY TURNED INTO DROSS OR LEAVES"--as if it followed that the conjuror's half-crowns really did become invisible and in that state fly, because he afterwards cuts them out of a real orange; or as if the conjuror's pigeon, being after the discharge of his gun, a real live pigeon fluttering on the target, must therefore conclusively be a pigeon, fired, whole, living and unshattered, out of the gun!--not because of the exposure of any of these weaknesses, or a thousand such, are these moving incidents in the life of the Martyr Medium, and similar productions, likely to prove useful, but because of their uniform abuse of those who go to test the reality of these alleged phenomena, and who come away incredulous. There is an old homely proverb concerning pitch and its adhesive character, which we hope this significant circumstance may impress on many minds. The writer of these lines has lately heard overmuch touching young men of promise in the imaginative arts, "towards whom" Martyr Mediums assisting at evening parties feel themselves "drawn". It may be a hint to such young men to stick to their own drawing, as being of a much better kind, and to leave Martyr Mediums alone in their glory.

As there is a good deal in these books about "lying spirits", we will conclude by putting a hypothetical case. Supposing that a Medium (Martyr or otherwise) were established for a time in the house of an English gentleman abroad; say, somewhere in Italy. Supposing that the more marvellous the Medium became, the more suspicious of him the lady of the house became. Supposing that the lady, her distrust once aroused, were particularly struck by the Medium's exhibiting a persistent desire to commit her, somehow or other, to the disclosure of the manner of the death, to him unknown, of a certain person. Supposing that she at length resolved to test the Medium on this head, and, therefore, on a certain evening mentioned a wholly supposititious manner of death (which was not the real manner of death, nor anything at all like it) within the range of his listening ears. And supposing that a spirit presently afterwards rapped out its presence, claiming to be the spirit of that deceased person, and claiming to have departed this life in that supposititious way. Would that be a lying spirit? Or would it he a something else, tainting all that Medium's statements and suppressions, even if they were not in themselves of a manifestly outrageous character?

THE LATE MR. STANFIELD

Every Artist, be he writer, painter, musician, or actor, must bear his private sorrows as he best can, and must separate them from the exercise of his public pursuit. But it sometimes happens, in compensation, that his private loss of a dear friend represents a loss on the part of the whole community. Then he may, without obtrusion of his individuality, step forth to lay his little wreath upon that dear friend's grave.

On Saturday, the eighteenth of this present month, Clarkson Stanfield died. On the afternoon of that day, England lost the great marine painter of whom she will be boastful ages hence; the National Historian of her speciality, the Sea; the man famous in all countries for his marvellous rendering of the waves that break upon her shores, of her ships and seamen, of her coasts and skies, of her storms and sunshine, of the many marvels of the deep. He who holds the oceans in the hollow of His hand had given, associated with them, wonderful gifts into his keeping; he had used them well through threescore and fourteen years; and, on the afternoon of that spring day, relinquished them for ever.

It is superfluous to record that the painter of "The Battle of Trafalgar", of the "Victory being towed into Gibraltar with the body of Nelson on Board", of "The Morning after the Wreck", of "The Abandoned", of fifty more such works, died in his seventy-fourth year, "Mr." Stanfield.--He was an Englishman.

Those grand pictures will proclaim his powers while paint and canvas last. But the writer of these words had been his friend for thirty years; and when, a short week or two before his death, he laid that once so skilful hand upon the writer's breast and told him they would meet again, "but not here", the thoughts of the latter turned, for the time, so little to his noble genius, and so much to his noble nature!

He was the soul of frankness, generosity, and simplicity. The most genial, the most affectionate, the most loving, and the most lovable of men. Success had never for an instant spoiled him. His interest in the Theatre as an Institution--the best picturesqueness of which may be said to be wholly due to him--was faithful to the last. His belief in a Play, his delight in one, the ease with which it moved him to tears or to laughter, were most remarkable evidences of the heart he must have put into his old theatrical work, and of the thorough purpose and sincerity with which it must have been done. The writer was very intimately associated with him in some amateur plays; and day after day, and night after night, there were the same unquenchable freshness, enthusiasm, and impressibility in him, though broken in health, even then.

No Artist can ever have stood by his art with a quieter dignity than he always did. Nothing would have induced him to lay it at the feet of any human creature. To fawn, or to toady, or to do undeserved homage to any one, was an absolute impossibility with him. And yet his character was so nicely balanced that he was the last man in the world to be suspected of self-assertion, and his modesty was one of his most special qualities.

He was a charitable, religious, gentle, truly good man. A genuine man, incapable of pretence or of concealment. He had been a sailor once; and all the best characteristics that are popularly attributed to sailors, being his, and being in him refined by the influences of his Art, formed a whole not likely to be often seen. There is no smile that the writer can recall, like his; no manner so naturally confiding and so cheerfully engaging. When the writer saw him for the last time on earth, the smile and the manner shone out once through the weakness, still: the bright unchanging Soul within the altered face and form.

No man was ever held in higher respect by his friends, and yet his intimate friends invariably addressed him and spoke of him by a pet name. It may need, perhaps, the writer's memory and associations to find in this a touching expression of his winning character, his playful smile, and pleasant ways. "You know Mrs. Inchbald's story, Nature and Art?" wrote Thomas Hood, once, in a letter: "What a fine Edition of Nature and Art is Stanfield!"

Gone! And many and many a dear old day gone with him! But their memories remain. And his memory will not soon fade out, for he has set his mark upon the restless waters, and his fame will long be sounded in the roar of the sea.

A SLIGHT QUESTION OF FACT

It is never well for the public interest that the originator of any social reform should be soon forgotten. Further, it is neither wholesome nor right (being neither generous nor just) that the merit of his work should be gradually transferred elsewhere.

Some few weeks ago, our contemporary, the Pall Mall Gazette, in certain strictures on our Theatres which we are very far indeed from challenging, remarked on the first effectual discouragement of an outrage upon decency which the lobbies and upper-boxes of even our best Theatres habitually paraded within the last twenty or thirty years. From those remarks it might appear as though no such Manager of Covent Garden or Drury Lane as Mr. Macready had ever existed.

It is a fact beyond all possibility of question, that Mr. Macready, on assuming the management of Covent Garden Theatre in 1837, did instantly set himself, regardless of precedent and custom down to that hour obtaining, rigidly to suppress this shameful thing, and did rigidly suppress and crush it during his whole management of that theatre, and during his whole subsequent management of Drury Lane. That he did so, as certainly without favour as without fear; that he did so, against his own immediate interests; that he did so, against vexations and oppositions which might have cooled the ardour of a less earnest man, or a less devoted artist; can be better known to no one than the writer of the present words, whose name stands at the head of these pages.

LANDOR'S LIFE

Prefixed to the second volume of Mr. Forster's admirable biography of Walter Savage Landor,[1] is an engraving from a portrait of that remarkable man when seventy-seven years of age, by Boxall. The writer of these lines can testify that the original picture is a singularly good likeness, the result of close and subtle observation on the part of the painter; but, for this very reason, the engraving gives a most inadequate idea of the merit of the picture and the character of the man.

From the engraving, the arms and hands are omitted. In the picture, they are, as they were in nature, indispensable to a correct reading of the vigorous face. The arms were very peculiar. They were rather short, and were curiously restrained and checked in their action at the elbows; in the action of the hands, even when separately clenched, there was the same kind of pause, and a noticeable tendency to relaxation on the part of the thumb. Let the face be never so intense or fierce, there was a commentary of gentleness in the hands, essential to be taken along with it. Like Hamlet, Landor would speak daggers, but use none. In the expression of his hands, though angrily closed, there was always gentleness and tenderness; just as when they were open, and the handsome old gentleman would wave them with a little courtly flourish that sat well upon him, as he recalled some classic compliment that he had rendered to some reigning Beauty, there was a chivalrous grace about them such as pervades his softer verses. Thus the fictitious Mr. Boythorn (to whom we may refer without impropriety in this connexion, as Mr. Forster does) declaims "with unimaginable energy" the while his bird is "perched upon his thumb", and he "softly smooths its feathers with his forefinger".

From the spirit of Mr. Forster's Biography these characteristic hands are never

---

1   Walter Savage Landor: a Biography, by John Forster, 2 vols. Chapman and Hall.

omitted, and hence (apart from its literary merits) its great value. As the same masterly writer's Life and Times of Oliver Goldsmith is a generous and yet conscientious picture of a period, so this is a not less generous and yet conscientious picture of one life; of a life, with all its aspirations, achievements, and disappointments; all its capabilities, opportunities, and irretrievable mistakes. It is essentially a sad book, and herein lies proof of its truth and worth. The life of almost any man possessing great gifts, would be a sad book to himself; and this book enables us not only to see its subject, but to be its subject, if we will.

Mr. Forster is of opinion that "Landor's fame very surely awaits him". This point admitted or doubted, the value of the book remains the same. It needs not to know his works (otherwise than through his biographer's exposition), it needs not to have known himself, to find a deep interest in these pages. More or less of their warning is in every conscience; and some admiration of a fine genius, and of a great, wild, generous nature, incapable of mean self-extenuation or dissimulation--if unhappily incapable of self-repression too-- should be in every breast. "There may be still living many persons", Walter Landor's brother, Robert, writes to Mr. Forster of this book, "who would contradict any narrative of yours in which the best qualities were remembered, the worst forgotten." Mr. Forster's comment is: "I had not waited for this appeal to resolve, that, if this memoir were written at all, it should contain, as far as might lie within my power, a fair statement of the truth". And this eloquent passage of truth immediately follows: "Few of his infirmities are without something kindly or generous about them; and we are not long in discovering there is nothing so wildly incredible that he will not himself in perfect good faith believe. When he published his first book of poems on quitting Oxford, the profits were to be reserved for a distressed clergyman. When he published his Latin poems, the poor of Leipzig were to have the sum they realised. When his comedy was ready to be acted, a Spaniard who had sheltered him at Castro was to be made richer by it. When he competed for the prize of the Academy of Stockholm, it was to go to the poor of Sweden. If nobody got anything from any one of these enterprises, the fault at all events was not his. With his extraordinary power of forgetting disappointments, he was prepared at each successive failure to start afresh, as if each had been a triumph. I shall have to delineate this peculiarity as strongly in the last half as in the first half of his life, and it was certainly an amiable one. He was ready at all times to set aside, out of his own possessions, something for somebody who might please him for the time; and when frailties of temper and tongue are noted, this other eccentricity should not be omitted. He desired eagerly the love as well as the good opinion of those whom for the time he esteemed, and no one was more affectionate while under such influences. It is not a small virtue to feel such genuine pleasure, as he always did in giving and receiving pleasure. His generosity, too, was bestowed chiefly on those who could make small acknowledgment in thanks and no return in kind."

Some of his earlier contemporaries may have thought him a vain man. Most assuredly he was not, in the common acceptation of the term. A vain man has little or no admiration to bestow upon competitors. Landor had an inexhaustible fund. He thought well of his writings, or he would not have preserved them. He said and wrote that he thought well of them, because that was his mind about them, and he said and wrote his mind. He was one of the few men of whom you might always know the whole: of whom you might always know the worst, as well as the best. He had no reservations or duplicities. "No, by Heaven!" he would say ("with un-imaginable energy"), if any good adjective were coupled with him which he did not deserve: "I am nothing of the kind. I wish I were; but I don't deserve the attribute, and I never did, and I never shall!" His intense consciousness of himself never led to his poorly excusing himself, and seldom to his violently asserting himself. When he told some little story of his bygone social experiences, in Florence, or where not, as he was fond of doing, it took the innocent form of making all the interlocutors, Landors. It was observable, too, that they always called him "Mr. Landor"--rather ceremoniously and submissively. There was a certain "Caro Pedre Abete Marina"--invariably so addressed in these anecdotes--who figured through a great many of them, and who always expressed himself in this deferential tone.

Mr. Forster writes of Landor's character thus:

"A man must be judged, at first, by what he says and does. But with him such extravagance as I have referred to was little more than the habitual indulgence (on such themes) of passionate feelings and language, indecent indeed but utterly purposeless; the mere explosion of wrath provoked by tyranny or cruelty; the irregularities of an overheated steam-engine too weak for its own vapour. It is very certain that no one could detest oppression more truly than Landor did in all seasons and times; and if no one expressed that scorn, that abhorrence of tyranny and fraud, more hastily or more intemperately, all his fire and fury signified really little else than ill-temper too easily provoked. Not to justify or excuse such language, but to explain it, this consideration is urged. If not uniformly placable, Landor was always compassionate. He was tender-hearted rather than bloody- minded at all times, and upon only the most partial acquaintance with his writings could other opinion be formed. A completer knowledge of them would satisfy any one that he had as little real disposition to kill a king as to kill a mouse. In fact there is not a more marked peculiarity in his genius than the union with its strength of a most uncommon gentleness, and in the personal ways of the man this was equally manifest."--Vol. i. p. 496.

Of his works, thus:

"Though his mind was cast in the antique mould, it had opened itself to every kind of impression through a long and varied life; he has written with equal excellence in both poetry and prose, which can hardly be said of any of his contemporaries; and perhaps the single epithet by which his books would be best described is that reserved exclusively for books not characterised only by genius, but also by special individuality. They are unique. Having possessed them, we should miss them. Their place would be supplied by no others. They have that about them, moreover, which renders it almost certain that they will frequently be resorted to in future time. There are none in the language more quotable. Even where impulsiveness and want of patience have left them most fragmentary, this rich compensation is offered to the reader. There is hardly a conceivable subject, in life or literature, which they do not illustrate by striking aphorisms, by concise and profound observations, by wisdom ever applicable to the deeds of men, and by wit as available for their enjoyment. Nor, above all, will there anywhere be found a more pervading passion for liberty, a fiercer hatred of the base, a wider sympathy with the wronged and the oppressed, or help more ready at all times for those who fight at odds and disadvantage against the powerful and the fortunate, than in the writings of Walter Savage Landor."--Last page of second volume.

The impression was strong upon the present writer's mind, as on Mr. Forster's, during years of close friendship with the subject of this biography, that his animosities were chiefly referable to the singular inability in him to dissociate other people's ways of thinking from his own. He had, to the last, a ludicrous grievance (both Mr. Forster and the writer have often amused themselves with it) against a good-natured nobleman, doubtless perfectly unconscious of having ever given him offence. The offence was, that on the occasion of some dinner party in another nobleman's house, many years before, this innocent lord (then a commoner) had passed in to dinner, through some door, before him, as he himself was about to pass in through that same door with a lady on his arm. Now, Landor was a gentleman of most scrupulous politeness, and in his carriage of himself towards ladies there was a certain mixture of stateliness and deference, belonging to quite another time, and, as Mr. Pepys would observe, "mighty pretty to see". If he could by any effort imagine himself committing such a high crime and misdemeanour as that in question, he could only imagine himself as doing it of a set purpose, under the sting of some vast injury, to inflict a great affront. A deliberately designed affront on the part of another man, it therefore remained to the end of his days. The manner in which, as time went on, he permeated the unfortunate lord's ancestry with this offence, was whimsically characteristic of Landor. The writer remembers very well when only the individual himself was held responsible in the story for the breach of good breeding; but in another ten years or so, it began to appear that his father had always been remarkable for ill manners; and in yet another ten years or so, his grandfather developed into quite a prodigy of coarse behaviour.

Mr. Boythorn--if he may again be quoted--said of his adversary, Sir Leicester Dedlock: "That fellow is, AND HIS FATHER WAS, AND HIS GRANDFATHER WAS, the most stiff-necked, arrogant, imbecile, pig- headed numskull, ever, by some inexplicable mistake of Nature, born in any station of life but a walking-stick's!"

The strength of some of Mr. Landor's most captivating kind qualities was traceable to the same source. Knowing how keenly he himself would feel the being at any small social disadvantage, or the being unconsciously placed in any ridiculous light, he was wonderfully considerate of shy people, or of such as might be below the level of his usual conversation, or otherwise out of their element. The writer once observed him in the keenest distress of mind in behalf of a modest young stranger who came into a drawing-room with a glove on his head. An expressive commentary on this sympathetic condition, and on the delicacy with which he advanced to the young stranger's rescue, was afterwards furnished by himself at a friendly dinner at Gore House, when it was the most delightful of houses. His dress--say, his cravat or shirt-collar--had become slightly disarranged on a hot evening, and Count D'Orsay laughingly called his attention to the circumstance as we rose from table. Landor became flushed, and greatly agitated: "My dear Count D'Orsay, I thank you! My dear Count D'Orsay, I thank you from my soul for pointing out to me the abominable condition to which I am reduced! If I had entered the Drawing-room, and presented myself before Lady Blessington in so absurd a light, I would have instantly gone home, put a pistol to my head, and blown my brains out!"

Mr. Forster tells a similar story of his keeping a company waiting dinner, through losing his way; and of his seeing no remedy for that breach of politeness but cutting his throat, or drowning himself, unless a countryman whom he met could direct him by a short road to the house where the party were assembled. Surely these are expressive notes on the gravity and reality of his explosive inclinations to kill kings!

His manner towards boys was charming, and the earnestness of his wish to be on equal terms with them and to win their confidence was quite touching. Few, reading Mr. Forster's book, can fall to see in this, his pensive remembrance of that "studious wilful boy at once shy and impetuous", who had not many intimacies at Rugby, but who was "generally popular and respected, and used his influence often to save the younger boys from undue harshness or violence". The impulsive yearnings of his passionate heart towards his own boy, on their meeting at Bath, after years of separation, likewise burn through this phase of his character.

But a more spiritual, softened, and unselfish aspect of it, was to derived from his respectful belief in happiness which he himself had missed. His marriage had not been a felicitous one--it may be fairly assumed for either side--but no trace of bitterness or distrust concerning other marriages was in his mind. He was never more serene than in the midst of a domestic circle, and was invariably remarkable for a perfectly benignant interest in young couples and young lovers. That, in his ever-fresh fancy, he conceived in this association innumerable histories of himself involving far more unlikely events that never happened than Isaac D'Israeli ever imagined, is hardly to be doubted; but as to this part of his real history he was mute, or revealed his nobleness in an impulse to be generously just. We verge on delicate ground, but a slight remembrance rises in the writer which can grate nowhere. Mr. Forster relates how a certain friend, being in Florence, sent him home a leaf from the garden of his old house at Fiesole. That friend had first asked him what he should send him home, and he had stipulated for this gift--found by Mr. Forster among his papers after his death. The friend, on coming back to England, related to Landor that he had been much embarrassed, on going in search of the leaf, by his driver's suddenly stopping his horses in a narrow lane, and presenting him (the friend) to "La Signora Landora". The lady was walking alone on a bright Italian-winter-day; and the man, having been told to drive to the Villa Landora, inferred that he must be conveying a guest or visitor. "I pulled off my hat," said the friend, "apologised for the coachman's mistake, and drove on. The lady was walking with a rapid and firm step, had bright eyes, a fine fresh colour, and looked animated and agreeable." Landor checked off each clause of the description, with a stately nod of more than ready assent, and replied, with all his tremendous energy concentrated into the sentence: "And the Lord forbid that I should do otherwise than declare that she always WAS agreeable--to every one but ME!"

Mr. Forster step by step builds up the evidence on which he writes this life and states this character. In like manner, he gives the evidence for his high estimation of Landor's works, and--it may be added--for their recompense against some neglect, in finding so sympathetic, acute, and devoted a champion. Nothing in the book is more remarkable than his examination of each of Landor's successive pieces of writing, his delicate discernment of their beauties, and his strong desire to impart his own perceptions in this wise to the great audience that is yet to come. It rarely befalls an author to have such a commentator: to become the subject of so much artistic skill and knowledge, combined with such infinite and loving pains. Alike as a piece of Biography, and as a commentary upon the beauties of a great writer, the book is a massive book; as the man and the writer were massive too. Sometimes, when the balance held by Mr. Forster has seemed for a moment to turn a little heavily against the infirmities of temperament of a grand old friend, we have felt something of a shock; but we have not once been able to gainsay the justice of the scales. This feeling, too, has only fluttered out of the detail, here or there, and has vanished before the whole. We fully agree with Mr. Forster that "judgment has been passed"--as it should be--"with an equal desire to be only just on all the qualities of his temperament which affected necessarily not his own life only. But, now that the story is told, no one will have difficulty in striking the balance between its good and ill; and what was really imperishable in Landor's genius will not be treasured less, or less understood, for the more perfect knowledge of his character".

Mr. Forster's second volume gives a facsimile of Landor's writing at seventy-five. It may be interesting to those who are curious in calligraphy, to know that its resemblance to the recent handwriting of that great genius, M. Victor Hugo, is singularly strong.

In a military burial-ground in India, the name of Walter Landor is associated with the present writer's over the grave of a young officer. No name could stand there, more inseparably associated in the writer's mind with the dignity of generosity: with a noble scorn of all littleness, all cruelty, oppression, fraud, and false pretence.

ADDRESS WHICH APPEARED SHORTLY PREVI-OUS TO THE COMPLETION OF THE TWENTIETH VOLUME (1868), INTIMATING A NEW SERIES OF "ALL THE YEAR ROUND"

I beg to announce to the readers of this Journal, that on the completion of the Twentieth Volume on the Twenty-eighth of November, in the present year, I shall commence an entirely New Series of All the Year Round. The change is not only due to the convenience of the public (with which a set of such books, extending beyond twenty large volumes, would be quite incompatible), but is also resolved upon for the purpose of effecting some desirable improvements in respect of type, paper, and size of page, which could not otherwise be made. To the Literature of the New Series it would not become me to refer, beyond glancing at the pages of this Journal, and of its predecessor, through a score of years; inasmuch as my regular fellow-labourers and I will be at our old posts, in company with those younger comrades, whom I have had the pleasure of enrolling from time to time, and whose number it is always one of my pleasantest editorial duties to enlarge.

As it is better that every kind of work honestly undertaken and discharged, should speak for itself than be spoken for, I will only remark further on one intended omission in the New Series. The Extra Christmas Number has now been so extensively, and regularly, and often imitated, that it is in very great danger of becoming tiresome. I have therefore resolved (though I cannot add, willingly) to abolish it, at the highest tide of its success.

CHARLES DICKENS.

The Codes Of Hammurabi And Moses
W. W. Davies

QTY

The discovery of the Hammurabi Code is one of the greatest achievements of archaeology, and is of paramount interest, not only to the student of the Bible, but also to all those interested in ancient history...

Religion   **ISBN:** *1-59462-338-4*   **Pages:132**
MSRP $12.95

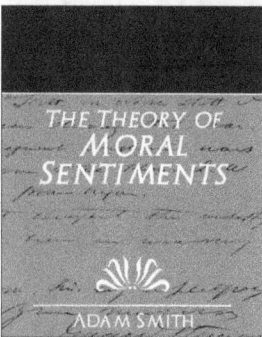

The Theory of Moral Sentiments
Adam Smith

QTY

This work from 1749. contains original theories of conscience amd moral judgment and it is the foundation for systemof morals.

Philosophy ISBN: *1-59462-777-0*   **Pages:536**
MSRP $19.95

Jessica's First Prayer
Hesba Stretton

QTY

In a screened and secluded corner of one of the many railway-bridges which span the streets of London there could be seen a few years ago, from five o'clock every morning until half past eight, a tidily set-out coffee-stall, consisting of a trestle and board, upon which stood two large tin cans, with a small fire of charcoal burning under each so as to keep the coffee boiling during the early hours of the morning when the work-people were thronging into the city on their way to their daily toil...

Pages:84

Childrens   ISBN: *1-59462-373-2*   **MSRP $9.95**

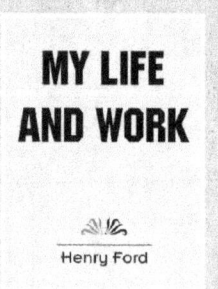

My Life and Work
Henry Ford

QTY

Henry Ford revolutionized the world with his implementation of mass production for the Model T automobile. Gain valuable business insight into his life and work with his own auto-biography... "We have only started on our development of our country we have not as yet, with all our talk of wonderful progress, done more than scratch the surface. The progress has been wonderful enough but..."

Pages:300

Biographies/   ISBN: *1-59462-198-5*   **MSRP $21.95**

www.bookjungle.com *email: sales@bookjungle.com fax: 630-214-0564 mail: Book Jungle PO Box 2226 Champaign, IL 61825*

The Art of Cross-Examination
Francis Wellman

QTY

I presume it is the experience of every author, after his first book is published upon an important subject, to be almost overwhelmed with a wealth of ideas and illustrations which could readily have been included in his book, and which to his own mind, at least, seem to make a second edition inevitable. Such certainly was the case with me; and when the first edition had reached its sixth impression in five months, I rejoiced to learn that it seemed to my publishers that the book had met with a sufficiently favorable reception to justify a second and considerably enlarged edition. ..

Pages:412

Reference   ISBN: *1-59462-647-2*   *MSRP $19.95*

On the Duty of Civil Disobedience
Henry David Thoreau

QTY

Thoreau wrote his famous essay, On the Duty of Civil Disobedience, as a protest against an unjust but popular war and the immoral but popular institution of slave-owning. He did more than write—he declined to pay his taxes, and was hauled off to gaol in consequence. Who can say how much this refusal of his hastened the end of the war and of slavery ?

Law   ISBN: *1-59462-747-9*   **Pages:48**
                                              MSRP $7.45

Dream Psychology Psychoanalysis for Beginners
Sigmund Freud

QTY

Sigmund Freud, born Sigismund Schlomo Freud (May 6, 1856 - September 23, 1939), was a Jewish-Austrian neurologist and psychiatrist who co-founded the psychoanalytic school of psychology. Freud is best known for his theories of the unconscious mind, especially involving the mechanism of repression; his redefinition of sexual desire as mobile and directed towards a wide variety of objects; and his therapeutic techniques, especially his understanding of transference in the therapeutic relationship and the presumed value of dreams as sources of insight into unconscious desires.

Pages:196

Psychology   ISBN: *1-59462-905-6*   *MSRP $15.45*

The Miracle of Right Thought
Orison Swett Marden

QTY

Believe with all of your heart that you will do what you were made to do. When the mind has once formed the habit of holding cheerful, happy, prosperous pictures, it will not be easy to form the opposite habit. It does not matter how improbable or how far away this realization may see, or how dark the prospects may be, if we visualize them as best we can, as vividly as possible, hold tenaciously to them and vigorously struggle to attain them, they will gradually become actualized, realized in the life. But a desire, a longing without endeavor, a yearning abandoned or held indifferently will vanish without realization.

Pages:360

Self Help   ISBN: *1-59462-644-8*   *MSRP $25.45*

The Rosicrucian Cosmo-Conception Mystic Christianity by *Max Heindel* ISBN: *1-59462-188-8* **$38.95**
The Rosicrucian Cosmo-conception is not dogmatic, neither does it appeal to any other authority than the reason of the student. It is: not controversial, but is: sent forth in the, hope that it may help to clear... New Age/Religion Pages 646

Abandonment To Divine Providence by *Jean-Pierre de Caussade* ISBN: *1-59462-228-0* **$25.95**
"The Rev. Jean Pierre de Caussade was one of the most remarkable spiritual writers of the Society of Jesus in France in the 18th Century. His death took place at Toulouse in 1751. His works have gone through many editions and have been republished... Inspirational/Religion Pages 400

Mental Chemistry by *Charles Haanel* ISBN: *1-59462-192-6* **$23.95**
Mental Chemistry allows the change of material conditions by combining and appropriately utilizing the power of the mind. Much like applied chemistry creates something new and unique out of careful combinations of chemicals the mastery of mental chemistry... New Age Pages 354

The Letters of Robert Browning and Elizabeth Barret Barrett 1845-1846 vol II ISBN: *1-59462-193-4* **$35.95**
by *Robert Browning and Elizabeth Barrett* Biographies Pages 596

Gleanings In Genesis (volume I) by *Arthur W. Pink* ISBN: *1-59462-130-6* **$27.45**
Appropriately has Genesis been termed "the seed plot of the Bible" for in it we have, in germ form, almost all of the great doctrines which are afterwards fully developed in the books of Scripture which follow... Religion/Inspirational Pages 420

The Master Key by *L. W. de Laurence* ISBN: *1-59462-001-6* **$30.95**
In no branch of human knowledge has there been a more lively increase of the spirit of research during the past few years than in the study of Psychology, Concentration and Mental Discipline. The requests for authentic lessons in Thought Control, Mental Discipline and... New Age/Business Pages 422

The Lesser Key Of Solomon Goetia by *L. W. de Laurence* ISBN: *1-59462-092-X* **$9.95**
This translation of the first book of the "Lernegton" which is now for the first time made accessible to students of Talismanic Magic was done, after careful collation and edition, from numerous Ancient Manuscripts in Hebrew, Latin, and French... New Age/Occult Pages 92

Rubaiyat Of Omar Khayyam by *Edward Fitzgerald* ISBN:*1-59462-332-5* **$13.95**
Edward Fitzgerald, whom the world has already learned, in spite of his own efforts to remain within the shadow of anonymity, to look upon as one of the rarest poets of the century, was born at Bredfield, in Suffolk, on the 31st of March, 1809. He was the third son of John Purcell... Music Pages 172

Ancient Law by *Henry Maine* ISBN: *1-59462-128-4* **$29.95**
The chief object of the following pages is to indicate some of the earliest ideas of mankind, as they are reflected in Ancient Law, and to point out the relation of those ideas to modern thought. Religion/History Pages 452

Far-Away Stories by *William J. Locke* ISBN: *1-59462-129-2* **$19.45**
"Good wine needs no bush, but a collection of mixed vintages does. And this book is just such a collection. Some of the stories I do not want to remain buried for ever in the museum files of dead magazine-numbers an author's not unpardonable vanity..." Fiction Pages 272

Life of David Crockett by *David Crockett* ISBN: *1-59462-250-7* **$27.45**
"Colonel David Crockett was one of the most remarkable men of the times in which he lived. Born in humble life, but gifted with a strong will, an indomitable courage, and unremitting perseverance... Biographies/New Age Pages 424

Lip-Reading by *Edward Nitchie* ISBN: *1-59462-206-X* **$25.95**
Edward B. Nitchie, founder of the New York School for the Hard of Hearing, now the Nitchie School of Lip-Reading, Inc, wrote "LIP-READING Principles and Practice". The development and perfecting of this meritorious work on lip-reading was an undertaking... How-to Pages 400

A Handbook of Suggestive Therapeutics, Applied Hypnotism, Psychic Science ISBN: *1-59462-214-0* **$24.95**
by *Henry Munro* Health/New Age/Health/Self-help Pages 376

A Doll's House: and Two Other Plays by *Henrik Ibsen* ISBN: *1-59462-112-8* **$19.95**
Henrik Ibsen created this classic when in revolutionary 1848 Rome. Introducing some striking concepts in playwriting for the realist genre, this play has been studied the world over. Fiction/Classics/Plays 308

The Light of Asia by *sir Edwin Arnold* ISBN: *1-59462-204-3* **$13.95**
In this poetic masterpiece, Edwin Arnold describes the life and teachings of Buddha. The man who was to become known as Buddha to the world was born as Prince Gautama of India but he rejected the worldly riches and abandoned the reigns of power when... Religion/History/Biographies Pages 170

The Complete Works of Guy de Maupassant by *Guy de Maupassant* ISBN: *1-59462-157-8* **$16.95**
"For days and days, nights and nights, I had dreamed of that first kiss which was to consecrate our engagement, and I knew not on what spot I should put my lips..." Fiction/Classics Pages 240

The Art of Cross-Examination by *Francis L. Wellman* ISBN: *1-59462-309-0* **$26.95**
Written by a renowned trial lawyer, Wellman imparts his experience and uses case studies to explain how to use psychology to extract desired information through questioning. How-to/Science/Reference Pages 408

Answered or Unanswered? by *Louisa Vaughan* ISBN: *1-59462-248-5* **$10.95**
Miracles of Faith in China Religion Pages 112

The Edinburgh Lectures on Mental Science (1909) by *Thomas* ISBN: *1-59462-008-3* **$11.95**
This book contains the substance of a course of lectures recently given by the writer in the Queen Street Hall, Edinburgh. Its purpose is to indicate the Natural Principles governing the relation between Mental Action and Material Conditions... New Age/Psychology Pages 148

Ayesha by *H. Rider Haggard* ISBN: *1-59462-301-5* **$24.95**
Verily and indeed it is the unexpected that happens! Probably if there was one person upon the earth from whom the Editor of this, and of a certain previous history, did not expect to hear again... Classics Pages 380

Ayala's Angel by *Anthony Trollope* ISBN: *1-59462-352-X* **$29.95**
The two girls were both pretty, but Lucy who was twenty-one who supposed to be simple and comparatively unattractive, whereas Ayala was credited, as her Bombwhat romantic name might show, with poetic charm and a taste for romance. Ayala when her father died was nineteen... Fiction Pages 484

The American Commonwealth by *James Bryce* ISBN: *1-59462-286-8* **$34.45**
An interpretation of American democratic political theory. It examines political mechanics and society from the perspective of Scotsman James Bryce Politics Pages 572

Stories of the Pilgrims by *Margaret P. Pumphrey* ISBN: *1-59462-116-0* **$17.95**
This book explores pilgrims religious oppression in England as well as their escape to Holland and eventual crossing to America on the Mayflower, and their early days in New England... History Pages 268

QTY

The Fasting Cure *by Sinclair Upton*   ISBN: *1-59462-222-1*   **$13.95**
In the Cosmopolitan Magazine for May, 1910, and in the Contemporary Review (London) for April, 1910, I published an article dealing with my experiences in fasting. I have written a great many magazine articles, but never one which attracted so much attention...   New Age/Self Help/Health Pages 164

Hebrew Astrology *by Sepharial*   ISBN: *1-59462-308-2*   **$13.45**
In these days of advanced thinking it is a matter of common observation that we have left many of the old landmarks behind and that we are now pressing forward to greater heights and to a wider horizon than that which represented the mind-content of our progenitors...   Astrology Pages 144

Thought Vibration or The Law of Attraction in the Thought World   ISBN: *1-59462-127-6*   **$12.95**
by William Walker Atkinson   *Psychology/Religion Pages 144*

Optimism *by Helen Keller*   ISBN: *1-59462-108-X*   **$15.95**
Helen Keller was blind, deaf, and mute since 19 months old, yet famously learned how to overcome these handicaps, communicate with the world, and spread her lectures promoting optimism. An inspiring read for everyone...   Biographies/Inspirational Pages 84

Sara Crewe *by Frances Burnett*   ISBN: *1-59462-360-0*   **$9.45**
In the first place, Miss Minchin lived in London. Her home was a large, dull, tall one, in a large, dull square, where all the houses were alike, and all the sparrows were alike, and where all the door-knockers made the same heavy sound...   Childrens/Classic Pages 88

The Autobiography of Benjamin Franklin *by Benjamin Franklin*   ISBN: *1-59462-135-7*   **$24.95**
The Autobiography of Benjamin Franklin has probably been more extensively read than any other American historical work, and no other book of its kind has had such ups and downs of fortune. Franklin lived for many years in England, where he was agent...   Biographies/History Pages 332

Name	
Email	
Telephone	
Address	
City, State ZIP	

☐ **Credit Card**   ☐ **Check / Money Order**

Credit Card Number	
Expiration Date	
Signature	

Please Mail to: Book Jungle
PO Box 2226
Champaign, IL 61825
or Fax to: 630-214-0564

ORDERING INFORMATION

web: *www.bookjungle.com*
email: *sales@bookjungle.com*
fax: *630-214-0564*
mail: *Book Jungle PO Box 2226 Champaign, IL 61825*
or PayPal *to sales@bookjungle.com*

Please contact us for bulk discounts

DIRECT-ORDER TERMS

**20% Discount if You Order
Two or More Books**
Free Domestic Shipping!
Accepted: Master Card, Visa,
Discover, American Express